ADVENTURES OF BENJAMIN BAXTER: BIRTHDAY BEDLAM

Book One of The Darkness Within Trilogy

EZEKIEL JAMES BOSTON

ELSEWHERE
E
P
PUBLISHING

Adventures of Benjamin Baxter:
Birthday Bedlam

Copyright © 2015 by Ezekiel James Boston
All rights reserved.

Published 2015 by Elsewhere Publishing
www.ElsewherePublishing.com

Cover art copyright © Bramasta Aji

Book and cover design copyright © 2015 Elsewhere Publishing

ISBN-13: 978-1-62538-051-7

Elsewhere Publishing
www.ElsewherePublishing.com

"You are asking the wrong question, Junior Apprentice."

"Am I?" Ben looked up to the moon in the clear night sky. This far from Las Vegas, the brighter stars pushed through the neon light pollution. His Master would say it was a good omen.

Tax answered, "Yes. You should be asking yourself, *Why is my silent setting so easily overridden?*" The robot paused in mock contemplation. "Perhaps you should have a word with your programmer..."

Even though no one would know, Ben pursed his lips to keep his amusement from showing.

Dedicated to:

Family & Friends
Mentors & Minions
Kay McGarvey

Ezekiel James Boston

The Adventures of BENJAMIN BAXTER BIRTHDAY BEDLAM

Chapter One

BIRTHDAY BEDLAM

UNUSUALLY BRIGHT, an early October full moon hung in the Las Vegas sky cutting light through the darkness of Meadows Towing sprawling junkyard. Benjamin Baxter edged to an intersection and placed a careful hand on the jagged kinks of flattened cars stacked twenty high and hoped his car hadn't already met the same fate.

He peered around the corner.

A light desert breeze worked down the long row of vehicles squashed and stacked like large Legos. The dry air pressed against Ben's face, bringing the heavy smell of rust and neglected plastic. Bathed only in moonlight, the true colors of the cars turned into muted tones. Shadows did most of the coloring here.

Doing his best not to break the silence that lay over the scrapyard like a warm blanket. Ben hurried down the row.

Movement at the far edge of the row caught his eye. He sucked in a quick gulp of air and froze.

This boar, like the one before, had long tusks, stood

waist-high and looked thoroughly pissed off as it crossed between rows of compacted cars thirty feet ahead. Ben eyed the spiked leather collar as it snorted and stalked.

He pulled out his new Anvilsmith tablet—a birthday gift from the Archon Primary Academy—and a spell card he'd crafted and programmed for a situation like this, and lined the SD card up with the slot on his device.

Ben kept the surprised gulp locked in his lungs. Like before, he hoped the boar would continue on.

According to the scry he had bought from Crystal, this was supposed to be a moonlit stroll through a vacant scrapyard to recover his stolen car. This guard animal, the second he had come across, signaled otherwise. Why'd they take his car in the first place? Better yet, what kind of lunatic would use ravished boars as guard animals.

He frowned. Worst sixteenth birthday ever.

If the operators of this lot were crafty enough to conceal the beasts from Crystal's divination, they were, at the least, starwise and, at the worst, well-practiced in the arts.

Ben let his breath ease out as the animal began to go around the corner.

His device gave a small tick. Ben's robotic companion—Tex—also searched Meadows Towing for his car and had just unsilenced his Anvilsmith. Unable to slide his finger to lower the volume and keep the spellcard ready, Ben pressed the tablet into his gut and prayed to muffled the speakers enough.

Loud and proud, Tex's synthesized voice blared, "Found it!"

The boar turned with a sharp snort and bristled.

Ben slid the spellcard the rest of the way in and pressed "activate."

The SD card shot from the Anvilsmith like a miniature black comet with a snapping green energy tail. It pulsed strongly with the same energy when it struck the ground.

His school tie and trench coat started to react to the pull from the sudden vacuum before the crackling energy shattered the card. It released a gust of wind, whipping Ben's coat and hair back when Orion, a large gorilla made of sparkling green energy, appeared from the destroyed spellcard. The magical glow faded as his conjured protector materialized.

Focused on Ben, its original target, the boar lowered its menacing tusks and charged. It tried to plow through the gorilla.

Orion dropped its center of gravity. Strong arms caught the boar and redirected on a tangent to slam into wall of smashed wrecks.

Ben was saved.

Orion fought on.

Ben felt the familiar tingling sensation at the center of his brain when the conjurer's link formed.

A rush of adrenaline surged through him as he piggybacked on Orion's awareness and the gorilla's senses became his own.

Together, they rolled with the force from the boar's charge. They had one of the beast's tusks in hand and beat at it with the other.

The boar got its feet beneath it and jerked its neck back to break free.

With a focused thought, Ben made Orion grab the other tusk. Before he could issue a follow-up command, the gorilla acted on instinct. A mighty yank ripped one tusk away from the creature's snout with a sickening crack.

Ben recoiled from the link and regained his own senses.

The boar's squeals of pain were cut short as Orion stabbed it repeatedly with its own tusk.

A chill ran up Ben's spine. His throat constricted.

Ben had summoned conjurations in the past to perform tasks around the Archon Private Academy. He had used this same gorilla to move Master Reynolds's heavy black cauldrons. There were joys in controlling creatures to do chores, but having conjured one who had killed filled him with disgust.

Orion thumped its chest in victory and sidled next to Ben, offering the bloody tusk to show it had completed the task set to it. Further, it tried to give Ben the mental reins to embody it again.

Ben shook his head at both the tusk and control. Appreciative of the gesture, he pet-patted the gorilla's massive hairy arm, but looked away in disgust. Between the rows of the compressed cars, his gaze went to the boar. He didn't want to see the dead creature, but his attention floated to the area.

Orion stood in the way, and Ben was glad his conjuration blocked the view.

"I said, *found it.*" Tex reminded him, its light metallic voice carrying through the Anvilsmith. "It is..." A ping sounded as Tex plotted coordinates. "Right here." That and a couple of deep breaths of the steel-laden air helped remind Ben of why he had come.

Ben turned his back to the boar and thumbed the volume down to 25%. He rubbed his face with vigor and tried to rid his memory of the crack and last life-ending whine.

"Need I remind you of how Master Reynolds will respond to your loss of a birthday gift on the night of its gifting?" Tex imitated Master Reynolds's Southampton accent. *"Lose one of your sixteenth's gifts, Benjamin, and you lose them all."*

Ben clenched his fist against failure. It would be the same as when he had lost one of the three gifts he received for his thirteenth birthday.

Most annoyingly, his third gift—Tex, a small Golemcast robot—was right. If he lost his car—a sleek, APA red convertible Transcend—Master Reynolds would demand he forfeit Tex and the Anvilsmith tablet.

No one ever had to surrender a second set of gifts. He'd be the grand fool of the APA.

Ben's brow pulled into a decisive knot. If he couldn't recover his car, he wouldn't return to school.

The dead boar had slipped back into his mind. Focused on the task, Ben swallowed the lump of bile trying to escape his throat. He took a steadying breath. "Tex, why do you always override my silent setting?"

"You are asking the wrong question, Junior Apprentice."

"Am I?" Ben looked up to the moon in the clear night sky. This far from Las Vegas, the brighter stars pushed through the neon light pollution. His Master would say it was a good omen.

Tax answered, "Yes. You should be asking yourself, *Why is my silent setting so easily overridden?*" The robot paused in mock contemplation. "Perhaps you should have a word with your programmer..."

Even though no one would know, Ben pursed his lips to keep his amusement from showing.

Tex knew Ben programmed his own gear. The robot had taken a solid shot at him. The hallmark of the Golemcast models was to analyze the assigned student and use the best associated method to challenge them to greater heights. Apparently Tex had pegged him for humorous sarcasm.

Aware that it would only be around a short amount of time, the gorilla pushed Ben's shoulder.

Ben nodded. "Tex, come to where I am and salvage what you can. Then, make an intercepting path to meet up with me."

Tex replied, "Will do, Junior Apprentice, but this is a scrapyard. There is a lot to *salvage*."

Ben groaned at Tex's response and pressed his lips tight to keep his biting reply in check.

Unlike his past two companions, Tex registered when he was snide to it. Even though Ben couldn't find the subroutine in Tex's code to prove it, he would bet anything that the small robot spitefully performed worse until plugged back into the mainframe. "Salvage what you can *from the spellcard* and combat Orion had with a boar in this vicinity."

A chime sounded. Tex noting his location. "Will do, Junior Apprentice, and will continue in stealth mode."

Even though Orion's time dwindled, Ben pressed *Modes* on his Anvilsmith and scanned the list presented. It went from *Silent* to *Survival*, and he noted his silent setting was still no longer active. He tapped it with a sigh and grumbled as he earmarked his next few programming sessions to create a *Stealth* mode. "Maybe that'll keep him silent."

Clearing the screen, Ben checked Orion's remaining time—three minutes. He tapped the timer and set a vibration reminder for when thirty seconds remained.

He then pressed Modes and Map. The Anvilsmith went blank for half a second. A top-down view of Meadows Towing appeared. Ben had created it from various Internet maps and modified it with what Crystal had told him. A green dot lit where Tex marked his car's location. A red dot marked where the boar's body lay.

Ben took control of Orion. Through the gorilla's eyes, he looked into dazed far off look of his vacant body standing there in full school uniform like he was lost simply lost in thought and not inhabiting a conjuration.

Using Orion's strong arms, he scooped his physical body close, and continued moving through the desolate maze. Two turns and five lengths of crushed cars later, Ben came across another boar.

He released his body, relinquished control of the gorilla, and was back in his own body before hitting the ground.

Having recently dealt with a boar, Orion made short work of this one in the same fashion. This time, it did not offer Ben the detached tusk as proof of its good work.

The tablet vibrated the reminder.

Ben considered pumping more power into Orion, but the least amount of time was for another five minutes and would pull ten arcane watts from the Anvilsmith's remaining ninety-five.

Having engineered a few devices able to store *awatts* from scratch and without guidance, Ben had become quite familiar with the measurement of arcane energy. A seven capacity laptop proved to be his top end.

Now he held a hundred in a tablet. Astounding.

As a matter of habit, Ben moved forward to have his hand in position to catch the small obdurium-steel strip that held Orion's memory from this casting.

Ben patted Orion's dense chest twice with a regretful smile. It saved him and battled for him. If it wasn't so expensive to keep the conjuration around longer...

The gorilla disappeared.

With a practiced flick, Ben caught the strip and pressed the obdurium into the base of the Anvilsmith. Amazingly, it backed up the data in five seconds.

Ben beamed.

His first tablet, a refurbished Tsuku model he had modified five years ago, would have taken ten seconds for each real-life second that passed. This badass tablet copied a minute per second.

Ben nodded his approval. "Nice."

Chapter Two

MEADOWS TOWING

A TWO-STORY AUTO shop sat at the center of the scrapyard. Across the second floor, above the six dark windows, squat fat letters spelled out *Meadows Towing*. Shadows filled the yawning mouth of the five work bays. Strange music, heavy on window-rattling drums and the sound of metal striking metal, screamed from the bays.

Though he'd expected something more formidable, the desolate customer waiting area—no less the maze-like columns of wrecked cars—made Ben doubt anyone ever came here, even during the day.

Like a gentle tug on his ears, the slight pull from the Inscription spell he had cast on the front fender directed his eyes.

Convertible top retracted, they had his Transcend up on a lift with the doors open. Gone was the standard, scintillating, candy red Archon Private Academy paint job. Matte black paint now covered every inch of his car.

Only a span of a hundred feet—without cover—separated him from his favorite gift.

Crouched behind the column of junked cars closest to the building, Ben pressed *Spells*. All the spells he had programmed during his time at the APA lay within the seven main categories of spell-type icons. He pressed the asterisk for enchantments. He tapped glowing eye icon for *Soul Sight* and noted options his old tablet never offered.

The old, one hundred and twenty feet max range now sat toward the left of a slider as the default position. The bar had thirty feet on the low end and topped out at six hundred. A second slider, duration, defaulted to a low of one minute, but could go out to ten minutes.

A ghostly image flashed behind his screen.

Ben fumbled the tablet and caught it. He'd forgotten about his addition of the animated background, and grabbed his chest. He made a mental note to change it to something less startling. He then slid the markers to the top end of the distance and duration bars.

The *Cast* button—which he had been so proud of when he designed it—looked like a burnt out neon sign. -50, the cost of the spell, lit behind it. Not part of the spell, red text appeared across the bottom of his screen. *This will decrease current capacity by fifty arcane watts. You will have forty-five arcane watts left.*

He smiled broadly before setting the spell back to the defaults. The note went away and usage dropped to one *awatts*. He'd have ninety-four left.

Ben remembered the emphasis of Master Reynolds'

annual commencement speech. "Never use more energy than you need."

He stood and hovered his finger over *Cast*. His pulse quickened. His stomach tightened. He tried to shake the nerves away, but like the memory of the tusk being torn from the boar's skull, his nervousness refused to leave.

Ben tapped the icon, and the Anvilsmith started shooting magical energy into his hand. Each mystic discharge resonated through his body, stronger and warmer than the last. The injections were at their quickest and strongest toward the end, and he realized he had forgotten to put his mouthpiece in only when his teeth chattered.

Ben preferred casting by SDs. The magic washed over and through him, but rebuilding the tiny spell cards was extremely time-consuming and quite expensive. Spells cast from tablets—as long as one doesn't mind having magic forced into them—were effectively free of material cost.

His eyes tingled as the power settled in his irises. There were no living creatures in the spell's range. He took another look at the windows for movement. None. He rushed across the opening.

In the garage, he felt the presence of three beings further in the building. If he could walk through walls, two were forty feet away and the other lay on the floor above him.

He looked toward the two on the ground level and focused his spell upon them.

Wall by wall, his vision penetrated the structure until he could see the shape of the two pale white outlines. Both were over six feet tall and built like professional football players. They had enlarged heads. He concentrated on their upward turned, pig-like snouts.

Involuntarily, Ben had held his breath. Since they wouldn't hear him over the blaring music, Ben dared to quietly exhale. "Orcs..."

Having read many stories about their greedy and violent natures, Ben searched for the control to lower his car so he could get out of there.

The main panel just inside the garage had several buttons and levers, but none of them looked to be what he needed. He moved over to the stall with his car and searched there.

The spell warned him of a presence, big and powerful, coming from along the outside edge of the building.

"Shit." Ben hustled up the lift ladder to his car and dove onto the backseat. "Shit. Shit."

Chapter Three

THE ORC MASTER

THE SPEAKERS BLARED the insane crashing music. Closer to where they rattled in their housing, Ben grimaced.

"Wha—" He lifted his hands away from the seat. The paint job didn't bother him so much, but if someone had ripped out his leather interior and replaced it with crappy vinyl. Unable to see in the darkness, he squeezed the cushion and didn't like what he felt or the plastic smell. "Someone's going to pay for this."

He shook his head. There'd be time to worry about that later.

Ben focused on the new presence closing in. It radiated power. A caster. Casters always registered stronger. His spell allowed his vision to penetrate the car door and the exterior wall to see a massive ten-foot body.

Its torso—longer and thicker than anatomically possible, even for orcs—connected to narrow hips. Its squat, powerful legs only made up a third of its height rather than half. The head sat thick on its shoulders like a short-snouted dog, and small horns rose just over its concaved ears.

Deep purple energy—Krotosian magic—emanated from the towering monstrosity.

The creature entered the work bays. It had to duck and turn sideways to squeeze into the building.

Ben caught a flash of light blue skin, a white t-shirt, and dark baggy jeans as it forced its way into the building. Voice deep and gruff, it barked.

The music shut off.

Its woofing continued.

Ben's ear picked out inflection and structure to the barking. Since his mother had refused to teach him her native tongue, he had approached Adept Yeffaux—the Archon Private Academy's Master Linguist—about learning Sylvan. Yeffaux's high eyebrows arched higher at the request, before snidely stating they don't teach *that kind* of language.

More than a hunch, Ben pressed *Options*, then *Translate*, and *To Text*. The Anvilsmith displayed Dwarven futhark. He knew Dwarven and this jumbled mess didn't read like it.

The Anvilsmith flashed *Orcish to English*. A number one appeared followed by a colon as the futhark morphed into English. "Why aren't you pigs out feeding the little pigs?"

A two followed by a colon blinked as a second deep, but not-as-gruff, voice answered, "They haven't been back in a bit. We figured they caught an intruder and are dining on fresh flesh."

"An intruder?" The massive teal creature asked, and

the Anvilsmith italicized *amusement* in parenthesis. "You two better pray your pigs left remains or you'll be honor battling tonight!" A pop-up window hovered over *Honor Battle.*

Honor Battle (v.) A ritual called by overlords pitting failed minions against each other in a fight to the death. The idea behind this outdated practice is to weed out the failures and grant the victor another chance to prove their mettle.

Two more white figures, more orcs, came into Ben's spell range from deeper in the building.

The four orcs jogged into the garage. Two Colon pointed at each. "You, go north. You, south. You, east, and I'll take west. Blow on your horn twice when you find something."

The four orcs separated to their directions.

Giving them a little time to get far enough away, Ben laid on the backseat with the Anvilsmith on his chest. Dark streaks and splotches lay on the ceiling. How did they manage to get oil up there?

The being on the second floor stirred. He'd almost forgotten about it.

Ben focused his spell on it and felt power radiate. Great, another caster. This one smaller, human-sized—a girl—and framed with Argosian red energy.

His head shook in disbelief as his spell ended. He could have sworn the girl's lips moved as if to say, "Help me."

It wouldn't be long before the orcs came across one of the dead boars. A part of him wanted to hit the button to lower the lift and peel out, but his starwise self knew he couldn't leave an Argosian in the hands of a vile Krotosian.

Ben tapped the rust-colored GC icon on his home row and whispered orders for Tex into the Anvilsmith, "Get here, get the car down, and be ready to roll." He then pressed *Modes* and *Survival* before Tex could reply.

Hoping, he tapped to *Pop*. The screen showed the effective radius of the weak teleportation spell. He grimaced. Just enough distance to get stuck between floors. No thanks.

Ben cued *Soul Sight*, topped the range out at six hundred, and pressed *Cast*.

His wattage tracker dropped to eighty-nine.

Twenty-six other life forms headed away from the building. He examined the cursory information. Searching, he wondered aloud, "Where'd the Krotosian go?"

His nervousness dissipated as he set his mind to saving the Argosian.

Ben climbed down from his car and entered the building.

They had built a kitchen into the customer service lounge and promptly neglected it. Odors of rotten cheese and rancid meat assaulted his nose before his eyes took in the slimy dishes piled in a sink. With each step something sticky pulled at the bottom of his shoes. The silver handle of a battered refrigerator, where it hadn't been caked over by muck, shone.

In a hurry to leave the nasty kitchen, Ben turned and entered the den. The smell worsened.

A disgusting, gray slab of meat hung from a hook in front of a massive hundred-and-three-inch television. Part of it resembled a rib cage, but the rest didn't resemble any animal Ben had ever seen. A legion of maggots worked the surface. Liquor bottles in varying stages of wholeness to shattered remnants covered the floor like mosaic tiles. Smashed glass formed sparkling mounds down the backs of the five battered sofas.

Given their relative cleanliness, Ben would bet the TV and four large concert-stage speakers mounted in the corners must've been new.

Two sets of stairs on opposite sides of the room led up out of the mess. Faint crunches accompanied each step as he moved to the closer one.

Buried under layers of crud and discarded wrappers, the staircase reeked with a sour tang. The center of every step had a sure, foot-wide strip of ground-in grime—except for the last two at the top.

He stopped short of them and leaned.

A business-quality wooden door stood to the left of the landing, while the right seemed to open into a hallway.

Ben considered the dirty and untrammeled stairs a moment longer.

All of these creatures' strides were longer than his, but something felt really peculiar about those last two steps. Though he hadn't taken anything from the Traps course offered by the school, the number of classes almost equaled the array that had to do with spells.

Not willing to risk the stairs, Ben put his mouthpiece in and cued up *Pop*. Noting the -20 behind the *Cast* button made of bubbles, he focused on the landing above the stairs, and pressed cast.

The Anvilsmith gave a magical shock.

He bit hard.

Another shock, and another, and another. *Pop* took

two seconds to cast and made all of his muscles tighten
—almost seizing—eight times.

Facing the wall, Ben appeared where he intended.
Sixty-nine *awatts* left.

The door to his left would lead to the room above
the car bays, but his knees turned to rubber and bladder
weakened upon looking right.

At the far end of the hall, in a room with dark shag
carpet, the hulking, light-blue-skinned Krotosian
monster faced him.

Chapter Four

THE KROTOSIAN & THE ARGOSIAN

THE AWFUL TANG from the stairs still filled Ben's nose. An acidic taste—fear—lit the back of his mouth when the creature's growl rumbled down the hall.

Ben faced it.

The creature dropped a turkey leg, snarled, showing jagged black teeth, and pulled a sword from over a shoulder as its pearl-white irises deepened to a hate-filled purple.

Focused on moving backward, Ben bit into his mouthpiece. His hand trembled. He tapped *Cast*.

Movement from the creature's non-sword hand called Ben's attention. Darkening wisps of lavender energy played around the creature's fingers.

Ben's Anvilsmith shocked magic into him.

Purple wisps floated around the monster's hand before it pointed and released a sinister blast of the woeful dark energy.

Ben flinched.

The hall disappeared. Darkness surrounded him. The air smelled of corn chips.

A smack hit the door, rattled the hinges, and pushed bright purple power through the cracks.

Forty-nine *awatts* left.

A horn warbled twice in the distance. Ben presumed one of the orcs must've found a dead boar.

Ben cranked up the brightness of the Anvilsmith screen and used it as a light source to navigate broken tables and furniture to get to the girl with the Argosian aura.

The door rattled violently behind him.

He reached out to the bag and his fingers lit on a shoulder through coarse material. Ben warned, "Be ready for a fall." He estimated the distance down through the floor. The backseat of his car would be right below them.

Ben bit into the mouthpiece and activated *Pop*.

The energy flowed through him and into the girl.

She shook from the seizing magic. Her teeth clacked eight times as power flowed through her and *Popped* her to the other side of the floor.

Twenty-nine *awatts* left.

A heavy lavender fog began to roll in from under the door.

Ben frowned at it and focused through the floor onto an area which should be above the driver seat.

The fog gathered and thickened.

Ben tilted in fascination. "Weird."

Two small, violet orbs—the eyes of the Krotosian monster—formed and glowered at him.

Ben activated *Pop* and bit into his mouthpiece as the Krotosian's top-heavy shape started to form in the fog.

Nine *awatts* left.

Ben dropped further than expected and banged his leg on the steering wheel.

Tex had lowered the vehicle.

"Thanks." Ben glanced to his little robot companion in the passenger seat, stole a quick glance to the still bagged, but rescued Argosian, and pointed to the ignition. "Jump it!"

Tex sprung over the center console. It slid its small hand into the keyhole. All the lights lit. The engine revved to life. "Done."

Ben slapped on his seatbelt and stomped on the gas. The tires squealed on the bay floor for a second before they caught traction. The Transcend shot out of the garage.

Shattering glass rang out behind them.

Ben checked his rearview mirror.

The Krotosian had plowed through the window and levitated in the air. Hovering, it scanned, found them, and flew to give chase.

Ben blew out a breath of air. He would have been in serious trouble if he was on foot, but the car easily began to put distance between them.

Energy began to form around the creature's hands as it gave pursuit.

The burlap bag spoke. "Undo my thumbscrews." Her voice didn't sound rough or monstrous. She actually sounded, normal. "I can help."

"No time!" Ben veered.

A purple blast kicked up dirt and rock.

Tex clunked into the door well.

Ben swerved again to avoid another attack.

The small robot slid under the seat.

They approached the edge of the scrapyard. Though he wouldn't admit it aloud, Ben yearned to see what kind of damage the Ram enchantment would do. "Alright, Tex. Get ready to hit the wall!"

His companion's voice came from the backseat. "My leg is stuck. I cannot get to the control interface."

Ben growled. This was exactly why he didn't think there should be a block between the driver and the car's systems.

The A. P. A. insisted that any student wanting to have their cars enchanted must have their Golemcast as an intermediary. If he'd had control, they would've been out of here already.

Closing on the perimeter, Ben eased his foot from the accelerator and checked the rearview mirror. The distant creature no longer fired.

Ben asked, "Can you reach her, Tex?"

"Yes."

He pumped the brakes, cranked the wheel, and drifted into a row which would lead to the front gate. Ben corrected the car. "Hey, bag-lady. Lower your hands to the floor."

She said, "My name is Penelope!"

"Okay." Ben shook his head at her demanding tone. "Penelope, put your hands toward the floorboard."

Penelope said, "They're there."

Ben could barely hear the fabric tearing as they raced through columns of bleak, destroyed vehicles. If she had this kind of attitude while being saved, what would she be like under normal circumstances?

Penelope said, "I'm not a bitch."

Ben wondered.

She answered, "Yes, I'm reading your thoughts."

He frowned. His knuckles whitened on the steering wheel. He wasn't remotely close to forming a true opinion of her and even further away from possibly voicing it.

Before he could voice his protest, she started casting. "Great sky spirits, lend us your ways." As though driving up a grade, the car rose into the air. "I'm controlling the elevation. You still control speed and direction."

Above the column of cars, color began to return to Ben's knuckles. He gave the steering wheel a slight turn. The Transcend reacted as though it gripped a road and eased left.

Moments later, they were higher than the wall and over.

He said, "We're clear. Whoa!" His body didn't press against the seatbelt, but Ben's guts and gonads felt like they'd stayed above the wall as gravity dropped the car toward the ground. The rapid descent slowed for the last few inches.

They landed like a feather set down by a soft wind.

Penelope climbed into the passenger seat. At near arms' length, she held Tex like a toddler with a messy diaper.

Tex had a long black strip of spiked leather—the salvaged boar's collar—wrapped thrice around its waist and shoulders.

Penelope wore the burlap like a dress. Her long, dark hair was matted with blood. Her legs, arms, and the parts of her face he could see sported wicked bruises and scabs from where her skin had been split open.

She sat and cut her blue eyes to him.

Ben put his attention back on the road.

"We need to make it to Pepperjacks," she offered without a verbal prompt. He knew she had read his thoughts again when she added, "No, I am not going clubbing. I know people there. They'll keep me safe until I can cross back."

"Will do," Ben replied and wondered what she meant by *cross back*.

She didn't offer and explaining.

He tried to mentally broadcast, *Stop reading my mind!*

Penelope turned away from him and pulled the mess of hair to shield the worst of her arms and obscure her face.

They were both silent on the drive back to the city. Expecting to be chased, Ben kept checking his mirrors for headlights in the dark. Surely there must be another working vehicle in Meadows Towing. Though the Krotosian proved too massive to fit any standard car, the orcs could drive.

Its voice less hollow at close range, Tex asked, "Are you going to disable the survival mode, or am I going to have to eventually override that, too?"

Ben lowered his Anvilsmith to the floorboard.

Tex hopped from Penelope to Ben, dropped to the floor. It checked the energy level. "Only nine arcane watts left?" The robot raised its face to Ben and shook its head in disapproval before looking back to the tablet. "Junior Apprentice, you should have conserved better than that."

Having not wasted a single *awatt*, Ben smiled before reminding his little companion, "And you said something about the survival mode?"

"Ah, yes." Focused on the Anvilsmith, Tex pressed *Modes* and *Normal*.

Normal. Ben considered the word. Tonight had been anything, but normal. He noticed his leg had started to bounce in anticipation. If Penelope truly knew people at Pepperjacks, he might be the first from the APA to enter the posh nightclub. He wouldn't mention a word about Meadows Towering to any of his schoolmate, but to actually make it into Pepperjacks... Would he be able to not share that?

Chapter Five

PEPPERJACKS

BEN STAYED hot on Penelope's heels.

So far, following her instructions had gotten his car valeted and him through Pepperjacks' stained glass front doors.

Something of a rite of passage, most underage casters tried to sneak into the private supper club, and his fellow Junior Apprentices often pointed out that he numbered amongst the few who didn't.

Ben noted each of those who had attempted as an untrustworthy slink. Why try to force your way into a place that actively tried to bar you?

Still, from their retelling of failed attempts, he'd already passed the first two hurdles that stymied most of his classmates. Self-conscious, Ben noticed his mouth watered in anticipation. Now, all he had to do—

Heady lavender incense snaked into his nose. It forced its way into his lungs and made his head spin.

The lobby he'd yet to observe went black.

All sound ceased.

He froze. First willingly, then he couldn't move.

A primal part of his mind flooded his body with adrenaline for a fight.

Forewarned by his classmates of what usually happened, Ben focused on keeping his wits. He swallowed the panic lumped in his throat. He'd thought Penelope could get him through. Apparently she didn't have as much juice as she thought. Well, unlike the slinks, at least he was invited. Penelope really didn't need him now anyway. She'd be safe.

He heaved a disappointed sigh. Having experienced it first hand, Ben understood how Pepperjacks kept their perfect record of keeping minors at bay.

Worry slid into his gut. What would happened next?

A tug on his sleeve guided him. Ben wanted to pull back and remain still, but found his legs in motion as he shambled behind the pull.

He'd heard stories of bouncers beating the crap out of people. Pepperjacks was supposed to be *the* place where magic could be openly discussed. They'd doubtlessly employ minotaurs, giants, or other physically powerful creatures for protection.

Given the light-blue skinned monster he'd encountered earlier, all of the things he grudgingly learned about at the APA—but hadn't ever seen—might actually be real.

A brick red curtain, trimmed with gold tassels, appeared in the darkness.

In front of him, a hand faded into existence pushing the heavy-looking curtain aside. A second hand, the other holding his sleeve, appeared. Then the rest of

Penelope faded into existence. She said, "Welcome to Pepperjacks."

Ben had imagined the club would be full of mystical creatures, dressed for a night out, gyrating to insane beats by a celebrity DJ.

Reality proved more disturbing.

Having slid through the weighted curtains, Ben marveled at the three story interior. On the opposite side of the large empty dance floor, a long bar lined a curtain-drawn stage. The masking lavender scent disappeared revealing the Pepperjacks' true succulent steak-and-seafood aromas

Ben exhaled his disappointment.

Contrary to the rumors, Pepperjacks seemed to be more of a dinner venue than a nightclub. Worse, the place felt entirely devoid of magic. He nodded. Even at near-maximum occupancy, it proved to be nothing more than a large, upscale restaurant.

Penelope released his sleeve, turned, and speed-walked between the two rows of crushed red velvet booths just on the inside of the club curtain.

Ben frowned and followed.

He checked each opulent booth they hurried past. No elves. No dwarves. No Halflings. No gnomes. Nothing special at all. Only humans chatting and enjoying their meals. He shook his head. Without the slightest hint of being starwise, even the patrons proved to be a complete letdown.

Was this what he had to look forward to after completing his magical education? Heck, the simple foyer at the Archon Private Academy alone held more mystique.

"Baxter!" An arm shot out from a booth. The hand grabbed his sleeve and reeled him. "What are you doing here?"

Ben tried to pull away.

The hand twisted, tightening the coat like a vice on his wrist, and pulled harder.

Ben knew the move well from school. How dare this mundane grab him? He stared death at the Asian man. The harder he stared, the quicker the facade faded. The Asian business man—suit and all—vanished, leaving an Archon Private Academy trench coat, like his own, covering the arm and torso. A blond man's harsh features and green eyes verified what his subconscious told him about the arresting twist of his sleeve.

Ben's anger burst. His jaw worked as he searched for words. "Uh, Senior Adept Collins—"

Collins' hissed, "This establishment is off limits to all Apprentices, including *Juniors*."

Ben wanted to break the grip. As the Senior Adept slowly articulated his title, Ben felt as though Collins dragged him through filth that would forever stain his skin with an irremovable stench.

The rumor of Geotheon Mossburg's—the student who successfully pulled away from Collins some six years ago—cruel punishments kept Ben from resisting.

The Senior Adept pulled Ben closer and asked, "How'd you get in?" Searching for an aura concealer, he patted Ben's waist. Not finding anything, Collins dug into Ben's pockets for any of the other enchanted totems that could do the trick. Collins pulled him a bit closer.

Held so, he had to lean over the booth, Ben extended his arm for balance. His fingers sunk into the plush velveteen cushion. Used to being frisked, Ben relaxed. He knew better than to offer a reply before Collins addressed him by name. And he worked on a good response.

Ben's his gaze fell on the Senior Adept's tablet. An Anvilsmith? The corner of Ben's mouth curled into a smirk. It was the same basic model as his own. All students under sixteen would kill for one. Ben had been gifted his, but an Adept—a Senior Adept? No, they should be onto something better, or, at the very least, have the Triforce model.

Collins patted the small of Ben's back. His hand then slid up to Ben's shoulders to check for a shadow harness. Ben had heard a demand for answers come from those clenched white teeth in the past, but this was the first time the depths of the Senior Adept's throat released a dangerous growl. "I asked you a question, Baxter."

About to answer, Penelope whispered over his shoulder, "Let him go."

Collins' hand popped open.

Ben couldn't believe how fast Collins' had complied. Even Master Reynolds had to repeat an order a couple of times when the Senior Adept locked his jaw. He took a step away from Collins and Penelope filled the space by his side.

The Senior Adept's lips were still pulled tight. His face taut with rage.

"He's with me." Penelope tugged at Ben's coat. "Enjoy your meal, you two."

A smile started to spread across Ben's mouth at the Senior Adept being told what to do when he noticed the person sitting across from Collins. She hadn't been there a moment ago.

Her white skin, veined with silver, looked as though she were made of marble. Deep crimson spiral tattoos covered the back of her hands from wrists to fingertips.

Ben tried to look at her face, but her high pointed ears stole his attention. An elf?

Penelope pulled him further away.

He didn't resist, but wanted to see more.

The oddity of Collins' dinner date disappeared in a shimmer as he and Penelope moved further from the table. Ten feet away, the woman appeared to be an Asian woman in a business suit sitting across from an Asian man in a similar suit — though the illusion didn't mask the man's locked jaw.

As he followed Penelope, Ben wondered how many people were paying attention to her bare feet, wounds, burlap dress, and mess of hair.

Everyone *appeared* to be eating and talking, seemingly oblivious to anything outside their booth. But if Collins and the elf were masked, what was really going on in the booths. As Ben focused to see past the illusion masking the diners; they started to shimmer.

Penelope pulled at his sleeve to keep him moving when he started to slow.

Chapter Six

THE PAINTING

THEY RODE in two ultra-slow elevators. Since they exit through a second door at the back, Ben didn't think actually moved at all. Their footsteps echoed as Penelope walked him the length of another long, warm underground hallway. Unlike the first, extensive murals covered this one's grey stone walls. The smell of the restaurant's delicious food had yet to diminish.

All the way down the hall, Ben tried to spot what filled the hall with light, but couldn't find a source.

They closed on a large antechamber. A set of massive oaken double doors were built into the far wall, rising further than Ben could see in the hall. Set in each door were more doors. One at thirty feet, another twenty, and the last at ten.

Penelope stopped him shy of the room. "Stay put." She hurried through the smallest set of doors. Why had she brought him this far only to have him stop? He tried to guess, but couldn't figure out a reason she didn't take him with her, or even into the antechamber.

Ben decided not to defy her. If Collins obeyed in an instant, he'd stayed put.

Soon, the largest set of doors, some forty feet high, caught his attention. There were a handful of things Ben had learned about in Mythic Monsters class at the Academy which could have need for the larger doors—cyclopes, dragons—but he hadn't paid much attention as, before tonight, he thought only humans existed.

Ben chuckled at his former naiveté. The Meadows Towing monster would probably love to have a set of doors he didn't have to squeeze through.

Waiting and waiting, he clapped his hands in arcs around his body.

Clap in front.

Clap in back.

Clap in front

Clap in back.

Ben heaved a slow sigh. "Lame."

Still clapping, he turned to the oil painting.

Though he'd traveled its ridiculous length, he still couldn't quite believe it stretched all the way back to the elevator.

A battle scene?

Ben examined further. All manner of creatures fought and cast spells in the mural. Keeping his feet planted, he stopped clapping and leaned closer. Conscious of slack loosening his jaw, he closed his mouth.

A female caster in ornate robes dedicated to an unfamiliar deity, hurled a fireball made of white power across the battlefield. Hisboian energy was supposed to be healing magic, but in this painting, she used the ivory energy to release one of the world's best-known offensive spells.

The battle looked to be white, orange, and red versus purple and black. He nodded to the two-sided battle. It only made sense that the good Hisbo, Vibros, and Argos casters would have banded together against vile users of Krotos and Nilos.

Doubt twisted his lips. He'd projected battle lines where he wanted to see them and uncertainty began to push against his assumption. Wanting to study more, he moved away from the antechamber. Halfway back down the hall, he switched to assessing a similar oil painting on the wall behind him.

He'd been wrong. He'd been really wrong.

Though this painting had many more fantastical creatures, both pieces of art showcased war.

War with no alliances.

War with no loyalty.

A whimper slid through his throat as the all-out-free-for-all-battle motif sunk in. He thought he'd only have to wait for his hue of magic to develop to be aligned with like-minded casters.

His skin crawled with disgust and he felt sick.

The dream—his dream—of being able to tell friend from foe upon observing a single spell cast to form an ideal allegiance with any caster of the same magic, burst.

Ben absentmindedly ran his fingers over the nine remaining SD cards along his left flank. They were his combat-related spells. Before, they'd given him a sense of security, now they felt woefully inadequate.

Having never heard of spells being cast with

Nilosian black, Ben had just started to focus on the casters and their spell effects when Penelope's voice echoed in his head from all directions. *Run!*

Ben tensed, ready to spring, but didn't know which way to go.

He glanced to the elevator, but whipped his head around the other way to where doors slammed shut with muffled thuds behind Penelope. The antechamber's threshold rippled prismatic waves as Penelope crossed.

Ben began backpedaling toward the elevator. She'd changed into jeans and a red, long-sleeved shirt, and her hair flowed free behind her.

The doors swung open again.

A tall, gangly, burnt-red-scaled creature, clad in a suit of black chainmail, chased after her. Large, bat-like wings unfolded from its back. It flapped once, lifted from the ground, and smashed into an invisible force at the threshold. Dazed, like a dog running into a sliding glass door, it crumpled.

Ben paused, pointed, and laughed.

His laughter slowed when the gruesome form registered. It looked to be a hybrid between a dragon and some other horrible thing.

The creature jumped back to its feet.

Ben stood three-quarters of the way down the hall speculating at the hybrid's other part. According to his books, it had to be a near-giant race. The bipedal, wide-mouthed monster he pictured in his head had an insatiable hunger which was rumored only to be outstripped by a want for violence. He tilted his head and guessed. "Tuzvul?"

Penelope urged him again, "Run!"

About to ask why, Ben motioned to the glaring dragon-tuzvul unable to cross the threshold.

A gargantuan red fist, as tall as the dragon-tuzvul, and covered in similar burnt-red scales, pounded open the smallest of the double doors sending them crashing from their hinges. In the same powerful stroke, the clenched fist slammed into whatever force kept the dragon-tuzvul from giving chase.

Air shattered away from the threshold in prismatic shards. The lighting dimmed and the hallway reverberated with a deep resounding *bong*.

Ben ran.

A muffled booming voice hiss-gargled two strings of syllables from beyond the door.

It didn't sound like anything Ben had heard. He couldn't imagine the alphabet, but figured the command wouldn't translate into *Tickle them*.

Running to the elevator, Ben pulled an SD and—angling his device upwards—slipped it into his Anvilsmith. Like usual, the infused item shot from his tablet like a comet, but the crackling green energy trail had a faint sizzling to it.

Confused by the extra sound, Ben stole a glance over his shoulder.

The large bald eagle spell card had shattered against the wall. Green shimmering energy clung to a fierce black-feathered fiend, which vaguely resembled the majestic bird of his planned conjuration.

It flew toward Penelope with menace as the tuzvul gained ground behind her.

Chapter Seven

BETWEEN TWO MONSTERS

A GHASTLY SCREECH, half eagle, half something from beyond, filled the hall. The usual casting chill ran up Ben's spine and settled in his brain before fading away. Unlike his gorilla spells, his eagle never handed over control.

He planted his feet and his dress shoes slid to a stop. Ben spun and willed the creature's reins to his hands. Ephemeral leather crossed his palms. He closed his hands.

The abomination resisted.

"Whoa." The reins ripped from his hands. Ben checked for rope burns in the dim light. "Where's my conjuror's link?"

The fiend flapped toward Penelope.

The dragon-tuzvul closed in behind her.

Ben extended his hands. The leathery material lay at the ready. He only had to close his hands. He waited.

The conjuration dove at Penelope.

Ben balled his fists and yanked hard toward the ceiling.

Commanded, the creature belted a defiant screech as its body rose and it shirked his control. It stretched its talons at Penelope.

She ducked.

It dove harder. Its talons glanced Penelope's shoulders, nicking shirt and flesh instead of digging into muscle and bone.

Penelope ground her teeth and didn't lose a step.

Having missed its first target, the eagle-based, black-feathered demon aimed its attack at the tuzvul. It scored as the creature's red scaled hand reached to snatch Penelope's trailing hair.

The creatures battled it out in the air.

Ben held the doors open.

His monstrous conjuration possessed greater maneuverability than the dragon-tuzvul. The demon-eagle arced and turned. Each time, it made several long ferocious slashes in the dragon-tuzvul's wing membrane, ruining the large monster's ability to maintain lift.

Penelope made it to the elevator.

Ben looked away from the fight to the elevator's flat brass control panel. "No buttons."

Penelope turned and pressed her palm against the brass plate. The doors began to close.

A triumphant roar brought Ben's attention to the dragon-tuzvul.

In a move reminiscent of Orion defeating the boar, the dragon-tuzvul got both of its clawed hands on its foe and rent a wing from the fiend's body.

Being magic, the eagle-abomination winked from existence.

The elevator doors closed.

Penelope focused on the wall.

Ben leaned to make eye contact. "What the Hell is going on?"

Her eyes dipped and glassed over on *Hell*.

Ben waved his hand in front of her face. Nothing. He pulled his other gorilla card and held it at the port of his Anvilsmith.

Given what had just happened to his eagle, he didn't want to conjure again. However, if the door opened to a dragon-tuzvul, his twisted conjuration would attack the closest living creature. He just had to make sure it wasn't them.

Nodding to his decision, Ben tapped his Anvilsmith settings and changed the *Conjuration Delay* from a tenth of a second, the lowest setting, to five seconds. Enough time to get distance from whatever unruly abomination came into being.

Ben pressed *Communicate* and *Companion*, then pressed *Modes* and *Map*. A faint ping signaled the tablet connecting. "We'll be coming out hot," he advised Tex. "Show me where the car is parked?"

A choppy robotic voice, not Tex, replied, "I do not know."

Though he knew the voice, Ben flipped the tablet over. The magical inscription he made by combining his initials with the school's gorilla mascot shone green on the device. It looked untouched. Ben asked, "Remy?"

"Yes." Rembrandt, Ben's companion before Tex, answered.

"Activate and ping the GPS Master Reynolds has installed in my vehicles."

Remy answered, "Will do."

One extremely active day with Tex, and Ben had forgotten how he had to spoon-feed commands to his former companion and how slow it talked. He added, "Add it to my map and contact back when done."

Remy answered, "Yes, sire."

Ben chewed on his lip and tapped *System*.

The elevator stopped, Penelope came back from her stupor and tugged on his coat.

He missed *Diagnostic* and hit *Restart*. The device pinged and began the shutdown sequence. For the first time, Ben felt the sting from always toggling *Never Ask to Verify* on his tablets. No verification made for faster casting—and, apparently, potentially dire accidents.

The doors started to slide open. She aimed for the narrow dark gap and tugged again. "Let's go."

Ben waited for the doors to open fully.

She gave an impatient sigh.

Another long corridor. This one without any illumination save a beacon of light at the very far end. Warmth poured an ozoney smell into the elevator. The elevator went dark.

"It's clear." She pulled him to walking, jogging, then running toward the light.

Ben couldn't help but wonder if there were paintings on the walls here, too. Fleeing a real monster, he shook the trivial thought away. "What the—" he paused to edit *Hell* out of the sentence in case it happened to be a trigger word for her. "What's going on?"

Penelope answered, "An assault on The Node!"

What the hell was a node? They never covered anything like that in school. He repeated, "The Node?"

"Yeah—" Penelope's tone held an *I know, right?* sound to it. "Nodes can be damaged physically and by magic. If destroyed, all spells in the region casted with the energy in The Key end. Worse, casters' magic would flag and possibly be—effectively—mystically neutered until they get close enough to an aligned Key." Her eyes widened as she took the explanation to grander scales. "It also dampens likewise energy around the world. Sometimes, effects can even ripple across dimensions."

She'd presumed he'd known what *The Node* was and thought he questioned how it could be attacked.

Region? World? Dimensions? While her explanation registered, Ben still wasn't sure what was going on or how The Key played into an attack on The Node.

About to ask the question another way, the true immensity of the attack occurred to him as they closed on the well-lit antechamber. Local casters of the type of magic in the key could be rendered entirely powerless. A bit selfishly, a small wave of relief chuckled from his throat. "So, this has nothing to do with my car then?"

The question stopped Penelope cold. She spun around with a gasp.

Ben pulled up short behind her. He hadn't caught her soapy smell in the elevator. His eyes went to the large inset oaken doors in the antechamber then back to Penelope.

Mouth agape, eyebrows raised, and eyes widened, she asked, "You're kidding me, right?"

Her offended tone turned his skin cold. He wished

they were still in a darker part of the hallway. Back there, he couldn't have seen her reaction and she wouldn't see the guilt on his face. Defensive about what would go through his mind next, Ben said, "Don't read my thoughts."

She turned from him to walk into the well-lit antechamber and motioned for him to come with her. "No need. It's obvious."

Head bowed slightly to avoid the stunned look on her face, Ben followed.

Still taken aback, Penelope shook her head.

He'd just wanted to express the Transcends' importance since he had just earned it—and his driver's license—a little over twelve hours ago.

She asked, "What is your name?"

"Huh?" Ben looked up to see her hard expression had eased a bit.

Penelope said, "Your true first and family name. What are they?"

Ben's lips twisted. Who still said *family* for last name? "Name's Benjamin Baxter."

She studied his coat. "Of House Reynolds?"

Ben exhaled. "I've asked you not to read my mind."

"Relax." Penelope turned to the door, knocked, and backed up to stand next to him. "It's the stitching that gives you away. Besides," she said, throwing him a wry smile when he glanced at her. "You've only barred *reading* your thoughts. You didn't say anything about *controlling* them." She mocked an over-the-top evil laugh.

At least Ben hoped she mocked it.

Chapter Eight

KOGRAKKEN

PRECIOUS MINUTES PASSED. Distant shouts, so faint Ben thought he could be imagining them, came and went. The hall behind them remained dark and the nested oaken doors before them remained closed.

He alternated between trying not to think—so his thoughts couldn't be read—and not sneaking a glance at Penelope. Her *tsks* had let him know when he failed either. Blessedly, his Anvilsmith vibrated as it powered back on. Ben put his tablet through a diagnostic check and smelled smoke. To make sure it wasn't him, he sniffed his tablet. It wasn't.

"I smell it, too." Penelope twisted to examine the corridor behind them. Worry worked at the edges of her calm voice. "I think the building is on fire."

Between keeping his eyes from scanning her contorted body. Her near casual tone almost missed her voicing his growing concern.

The handle on the second inner set of doors rattled, then opened. A bald giant, in full plate armor with a helmet tucked under his arm, had to duck his head to get through the twenty-foot-tall door. The giant closed the door behind itself, slid its rear tree trunk leg back and considered them.

Ben's insides tightened and shook. Reflexively, he leaned back and had to fight the desperate urge to run. This was the first giant he'd ever seen, and he barely stood taller than its knees. Being this close made him feel quite small.

It heaved a ragged breath.

Though his nerves began to settle, Ben had to fight to keep the vision of being punted halfway down the hallway from dominating his thoughts.

A giggle from Penelope let him know he failed.

Ben ground his teeth and projected. *Stop that!*

She chuckled and projected back. *Stop thinking so loudly.*

Though upset with her, he found a smile on his face. Her infectious mirth had traveled a tenuous telepathic bond between them.

The giant's face turned sour. Larger than both of them, it changed the mood and set the tone. It nodded to Penelope. "You may pass."

Ben winced. His ears rang from the sheer volume of the giants booming voice.

It focused on Ben. "I do not recognize him."

Penelope said, "He is Benjamin Baxter of House Reynolds."

The giant nodded and lowered his voice. "The House is respected well enough, but this one is still stitched in Junior Apprentice robes."

Ben bristled at his title, but then calmed. The giant

didn't judge him for being a Junior Apprentice, it merely stated what its large eyes observed. He decided to correct the giant just the same. "It's a trench coat."

It looked back to Penelope. "Sorry, Junior Miss. He must wait."

Ben rolled her title in his head. He knew all the ranking titles of local schools and covens. None of them tracked their practitioners' with *Miss*.

Penelope said, "Kograkken, The Node is under attack."

The giant's eyes went from them to down the hall. It pulled out a sword the length of a small car.

Ben took a tentative step back.

"Then he will prove his mettle with me in The Hall." Kograkken swung a couple of practice arcs and bent at the knees as though he braced to catch something. "Afterwards, The Painting will show if he is worthy. Then, and only then, will I let Baxter-Reynolds through."

The Node, The Key, The House, The Hall and now *The Painting*. Ben tried to keep his smile inwards as he wondered where *The Bathroom* could be.

Penelope gave Ben a brief disappointed gaze before pointing over his shoulder. "He's already there."

"I am?" Ben turned.

The giant's shadow fell over him as it followed her point.

There, in oil at the edge of the painting as though he belonged in the battle. With his Anvilsmith in hand, The Painting had him controlling the black-eagle fiend as it faced-off with the dragon-tuzvul.

Ben smiled at his likeness. Whoever did this

absolutely captured the way conjurations always blew his hair and coat back. "Heh, look at that." He leaned a bit closer and frowned at the black magic reins between him and the demon-bird.

Kograkken must've seen it too. The giant roared. "Nilosian!" The giant whacked him.

"Oof!" Ben's air burst from his lungs and through his lips from the surprise blow.

Stunned, first by the giant's booming voice then by its backhand, Ben found himself laid out on the ground. An ache played on the left side of his body—where he'd been whacked—for a moment before quickly settling in his bones. A dull throbbing from the rough landing filled his right shoulder.

Ben tried to recover his breath.

Kograkken slipped the blade's thin tip under his chin. "What have you to say before you die?"

Still gasping for air, Ben looked to Penelope for help.

She moved to the painting to study it.

Ben scrambled backward on the stone floor.

Kograkken matched his retreat with steady platemail rattling strides while keeping the sword at Ben's throat.

Penelope's eyes shot wide. Absolutely transfixed by what she saw, she covered her mouth.

As his thoughts raced, Ben realized that the only time he had ever heard of Nilosian casters in the past were when they had been uncovered and—to his thinking then—rightfully slain. Ben blurted, "I'm colorless!"

Kograkken continued after him. "Lies."

Ben continued to shuffle back. "Someone must've

swapped out my spell cards." The top of his head hit stone.

Kograkken kept the sword steady, pinning Ben against the wall with his stare as well as the tip of his blade. "Junior Miss?" The giant's head turned slightly, but those large eyes stayed on Ben. "Your orders?"

Why had his formerly pure green magic turned black? Ben's mind went back to when Senior Adept Collins had frisked him for an aura concealer. The jerk must've done something to him. Ben's brow furrowed at the betrayal. He never liked the Senior Adept, but this was some serious bullshit and now he might be killed.

Hand by his side, Ben snapped his fingers and his eyes widened. "Check my aura!" The regular disappointment his mother tried to keep secret when he had cast at home would be his saving grace. "Either of you." He failed to keep the desperation from his voice. "It'll show what I am."

Kograkken twisted his hilt. The sharp tip swiveled under Ben's chin. The metal began to take on a green hue. The giant pulled the blade away when the faint seafoam tinge darkened to a solid emerald.

That close to being killed, Ben used the smooth stone wall to stand, and rested against it. His whole body was shaking.

"Baxter-Reynolds." Kograkken towered over him and leaned further until it loomed close. "Those who use the darkest magic deserve the worst deaths."

Being found innocent of not being a Nilosian, and being allowed to live, Ben glared at the giant. Vindication gave him a bit of moxie. He straightened his trench coat, dusted the shoulders, and waited for an apology.

Kograkken sneered and repeated, "*The worst deaths.*"

A light ding, that of the elevator, traveled the hall. Penelope hustled to the doors. "Come on."

The giant put on its helmet.

Ben followed behind her and stopped at the door. "I'm colorless"

Kograkken's focus lay at the far end of the hallway. Faint frenzied screams and roars grew in strength. The giant gave his sword two more warm-up swings.

Leery of the giant taking another cheap shot, Ben walked backward through the door.

Before it closed, Kograkken whispered, "For now."

Chapter Nine

CASTING TROUBLE

As THOUGH TIMED with the warm golden sunlight coming through the chunky one-foot-square windows, the smell of delicious, freshly-baked bread grew in intensity. Savoring the scent, Ben took in another deep breath. His stomach growled. He'd have to find the bakery.

Shuffling feet behind him raised his hopes. Maybe Penelope had finally come back for him.

The wide hallways on this side of the door were equally as long as the ones on the other side, but red marble had replaced the dreary granite. The walls here arched in a ceiling some twenty feet overhead.

Instead of long murals, paintings of wizards in gold and crimson robes peppered the walls at ten foot intervals. As much as the magic battle royal bothered him, Ben would much rather study the spells being cast than try to guess the rank of the people in the portraits. Though they were stock still, it started to feel like they disapproved of him being there.

If only the hallways were shorter; there'd be less of them to make him feel like an interloper.

As with the few other folks he'd seen. The person coming from the corner also wore red robes. This one proved too tall to be Penelope.

When she left him, Penelope said he could explore, but there was only so many red-marbled halls filled with hundreds of portraits one could look at...

"Just don't leave the building." Ben quietly mocked her voice. He heaved a sigh. "Like I could get out."

Not for the first time, the fatigue of being up all night began to press upon him. Ben yawned and tried to stretch his weariness away.

He approached another one of the thickly set clear windows centered between the portraits, but—as though it could tell his intent to look out and judge his proximity—the glass grew cloudy and opaque as he neared to gaze upon the outside world.

Ben shook his head. "Lame."

A portrait grabbed his attention.

Nearly all of the people in the other painting were much older than him, but the boy in this one looked to be no older than Ben was when he became an Initiate at the Archon Private Academy six years ago.

The kid's eyes were so bright and joyful that Ben felt his own spirits lifting.

"Five more years." Ben spoke to the portrait about what would bring joy to his own heart. "Then I won't need an escort. I'd be able to go anywhere. Paragon Casino. Geyser Palace. Pepperjacks..."

The robed person who passed Ben stopped, his light voice alive with interest. *"Pepperjacks,* you say?"

Ben turned to see a male version of Penelope about to pass him. He stood a good ways over six feet tall, much taller than Ben, and had his waist-length dark hair hanging in twin braids in front of his shoulders. He wore red robes similar to what Ben presumed were the lower-ranked people in the portraits. Ben nodded. "Yeah."

"You pronounce the name like all the others from your side do." The guy's smooth voice held regal intonations. "This leads me to wonder, does anyone over there actually read the sign in front of the building?"

Thinking back, Ben could readily recall the logo, but not the words underneath.

The man looked him over. "The proper name is, truly, *Pepper & Jack's*." He leaned in a slight bow and extended his hand with his fingers spread wide apart. "And I should know, for I am Jack."

Hesitant to engage in conversation—she didn't say not to talk to anyone—with this guy, Ben's trench coat parted when he offered his own hand. "Name's Ben."

Jack's eyes dropped to the Anvilsmith and SD cardholder on Ben's waist. They widened. He smiled before reestablishing eye contact. "So, you are the one who rescued Pepper from the Ogre's camp?"

Figuring *Pepper* was a childhood nickname, Ben angled at a clarification. "If by Pepper, you mean Penelope..."

Jack's eyes darted to the right before nodding.

Ben nodded in return. "Then, yes."

Jack brought his hand back and extended it perpendicular to his body. He bent at the hip and swept it across his body at the shoulder. His hand barely missed the floor as he executed a *deep folding bow* with perfect form. "You have our family's deepest gratitude and, rest assured, you will be rewarded handsomely."

Jack's fluid moves triggered a bit of envy.

Adept Matton had given Ben an Unsatisfactory in Courtmanship V last eighth. The last prereq to the rest of the Spell Programming curriculum, Ben needed to retake it—and pass—next eighth to keep his record setting advancement.

Only if Matton allowed tutors for his classes, or gave pointers outside class hours. Ben would then only need pass Spell Programming IX and X to become a permanent part of APA history for being the fasted to advance through Programming. Anyone else could only tie him. Almost able to taste it, Ben licked his lips. As much as Jack's presence made him uneasy, he could learn a great deal by just being observant of the wizard's actions.

Jack, still bent low, commented. "I see you carry an Anvilsmith."

Ben placed his hand over his trench coat and protectively pressed the device against his body. "Just got it."

"For saving my sister," Jack said, still folded in half and speaking to his own knees, "I am certain my father will reward you with nothing less than a Sunforge."

Avid about tablets, Ben looked up and slowly shook his head. No such thing as a *Sunforge*. "I haven't heard of—"

Ben looked at Jack to see him still fully bent. He growled at his huge breach of etiquette. Matton would've had him stand with his nose in the corner—like a misbehaved child—and given him detention. Ben brought the heels of his dress shoes together.

Upon hearing the slight clack, Jack unbent. He barely drew breath.

Ben's envy turned into admiration. Bending that far always taxed him and he couldn't help but draw a deep refreshing drag of air after being granted permission to stand upright. Inwardly, he reaffirmed his vow of working on the move when alone.

Yeah, he could use all of Jack's fluid moves as a primer. Ben kept a keen eye out for the small moves Adept Matton drilled.

From Jack, they flowed naturally.

Ben shook his head and continued his earlier thought. "There is no such device."

"On your side." Jack gave a sly smile. A perfect flip of the wrist turned Jack's hand palm up and he brought it close to his body. "Over here, we have our own makers." With a sweep of his arm, Jack gave another flawless courtly gesture for Ben to walk with him.

Obligated by politeness, Ben did.

"Though it may not be as good as your Master's tablet—" Jack gave a subtle shrug as if to rhetorically ask *what could.* "—it far out strips all Anvilsmiths—even the touted *breakthrough* Triforce model from last year."

Though Jack wore robes of a traditionalist, he knew his stuff when it came to the tools of technocasting.

Hungry to have an even better tablet, and items that would further enhance his casting ability, Ben wondered what other gadgets he could get his hands on over here.

They talked and walked. Jack went to lead Ben
down a series of red-marbled stairs. Glad to have
company, Ben went, but kept Penelope's instructions in
mind. He'd let Jack give him a tour, but would draw the
line at leaving the building.

Chapter Ten

SIDEWAYS, NOT DOWN

BEN LICKED HIS LIPS. Not only were they getting closer to the bakery, but, very soon, the weight of a vastly superior tablet could grace his hip. When he got it, should he keep the device hidden or parade it around?

Both options had their pros and cons. Most students often showed off their new stuff and ridiculed others for not having the latest and the greatest.

He'd have something none of them could possess. Ben braced himself against becoming one of *them*.

Instead of letting his possessions define him, he'd do something of worth, something they—even if they could do it all over again—couldn't do. Completing all ten levels of Spell Programming with half a year to spare before first graduation would do the trick.

He'd keep the Sunforge strapped to the small of his back. Ben wanted to give a portrait a knowing nod, but there were none around.

Somewhere along the way, the hall color changed from red to gold and then to orange. Their footfalls, particularly his hard soles, made a bit more noise as though he were walking through the APA's marbled main entrance.

He began to feel a kinship with Jack. They both were fascinated with tablets.

Jack's eyes lit as he talked about the different devices.

Ben often felt he bored his fellow Junior Apprentices when he went on a streak comparing the various models. Jack was more than game.

In fact, there were times when Jack rattled continually about how *his side's* tablets matched up against *Ben's side*. From the sounds of it, besides a small handful of Gnomecraft models, the majority of stuff available here surpassed comparable tablets Ben had once fantasized about owning.

Ben smiled at the thought of Senior Adept Collins making him pull the superior tablet during Spell Mastery IX. The look on the blond jerk's face would be priceless.

When it came to remembering the various specs of the myriad of devices—for the first time—Ben felt he met his superior. Given access to the same information, he'd be able to catch up, but it was possible that Jack's passion for tablets just might outstrip his own.

About to ask about the *Ivory Chain* tablet Jack named as top of the line, Ben thought of Collins again. A different question came to mind. He rubbed his hands together. Knowing this would be the decisive point of how to rank his forthcoming Soulforge. "What do Senior Adepts use on this side?"

"Senior Adepts?" Jack gave the title some thought

and motioned Ben through another archway with him. "We do not have Senior Adepts on our side. Like the various other comparisons we have been making, our titles are different."

Ben nodded. Made sense. He raised a finger into interject.

Jack continued, "A Senior Adept would be somewhat comparable to our High Magus."

Ben said, "Why—"

Refusing to be derailed, Jack continued, "They would absolutely refuse to touch anything less than a Triforce." A quick reflexive motion, almost mistakable for a twitch worked the corner of Jack's nostrils. Coupled with the flare, his nose lifted up to the ceiling ever so slightly. "If they touched an Anvilsmith at all."

Adept Matton's words came back to Ben. "*A master courtier never shows even the slightest distaste.*" He nodded to the memory. Jack proved to be a good model, but gratefully he wasn't faultless. The pressure of having to become as perfect as Jack eased.

Still, Ben smiled greedily.

If Adept Matton found out how he came across the tablet, his teacher would be sorely disappointed with him for accepting a reward for doing a good deed, but —no doubt—the Soulforge would be impossible for him to turn down.

"All right." Ben took advantage of the lull in the conversation. "Quick non-related question—" He eased into a smile to keep his shameful greed from showing. "—why do you keep making distinctions between *sides*?"

Seemingly lost, Jack blinked at him.

Ben wanted to punch himself for asking such a stupidly basic question.

"Well," Jack seemed to recover. "Sides of the portal, as in the two sides of the dimensional door at *Pepper & Jack's* guarded by the giant."

Why didn't he refer to Kograkken by name as Penelope had?

Ben looked back the way they'd came. A mild fear took root knotting his stomach. Talk about being stupid. He'd followed Penelope, a girl he didn't really know, to a very unfamiliar place. Now, he'd wandered off with someone entirely new, with no idea as to how he would get back to where Penelope had left him.

The portrait-filled red marbled hallways had gone away a while ago. Ben tried to recall the color of the halls between them and the cold gray stone passageway where he and Jack now stood. Coming up short, he took inventory of his surroundings.

Wanting food, he'd been absent-mindedly following Jack toward the fresh bread smell. While it increased in potency, the hallway had cooled. He found his arms folded across his chest for warmth. Torches lit the icy stone hallway. Their light barely threw shadows to meet with the next sconce and the weak fires did nothing to dispel the chill sinking into his heart.

"Pepper... I mean," Jack's eyes darted to the right again. He corrected himself, "Penelope did not tell you?"

Uncertain of what he should've been told, Ben came to a stop and shook his head. "She didn't tell me much of anything, really."

Jack's smile held a *we both know that's not true* feel. "Surely she told you to stay in the building."

Ben nodded. He motioned to the way they'd came. "Are we still in the building?"

"Oh yes." Condescension filled Jack's snicker.

Ben kept his annoyed reaction in check.

Jack didn't seem aware of his own laugh. He sniggered a little longer then gave a palm-up *walk with me* motion again. This one wasn't so smooth; it would have only barely gotten a passing mark in Courtmanship I or II. Jack said, "The Suntouched Spire has a great deal of underground—"

Spires rose high into the air. They'd gone down for a long while. The more Ben thought about it, they'd stopped descending a while ago and had been walking these gray hallways for about an equal amount of time. Ben's nape hairs began to rise.

Another quick snicker slipped from Jack.

Ben whispered, "Kograkken."

"Of course." Jack replied, but looked lost.

Ben took a small step away. Laughter aside, he could no longer ignore Jack's worsening etiquette. That and the fact Jack didn't know the giant's name was too much. His eyes narrowed and he jutted a thumb over his shoulder. Ben asked, "Why haven't we seen anyone el—?"

Hands aimed at Ben's tablet and SD cardholder, Jack lunged.

Chapter Eleven

FALSE FRIEND

FOR SOME REASON, a line from Julius Caesar went through Ben's head. *Et tu, Brute?* They'd made serious study of the Shakespearian play during Ego Control III. Ben thought the ultimate lesson to be learned from the class was about not letting power corrupt. Now he understood Adept Mong's closing lecture about Brutus' loyalty and eventual betrayal.

The thought caused him to hesitate. By the time he'd recoiled, Jack's hands were already inside his coat, both on their intended targets.

Ben grabbed the slack of red robes around Jack's wrist. As Senior Adept Collins often did to him—and many other students—Ben twisted, turned, and rotated at the hips

Jack's hand popped open.

In flurry of red flapping robes, Ben sprawled Jack on the floor.

Jack's other hand still clutched Ben's SD cardholder.

One of his cards flew free when Jack smacked flat on his back. It skittered to a quick stop.

With a twist of his own wrist, Jack slipped from the robes revealing a myriad of tattoos all over his torso.

Ben lunged for his cards.

Jack pulled his prize in tight and called, "Up!"

The air around them rippled. Warm arcane energy brushed by Ben to close on Jack.

Jack flashed with purple Krotosian energy. He went from prone to standing.

Ben grabbed one of Jack's braids. He went to pull the thief down and was left holding a wig.

Jack laughed as he raced down the hall.

Ben scooped up the card left behind and gave chase. He warned, "They're cursed!"

"Ev'n cursed," Jack's well-paced tones were now broken into a barely understandable cant. "These'll fetch a Barron's trove."

A fast runner, Jack pulled a little further away.

Ben noticed a larger shape formed from the dozens of smaller tattoos on Jack's back—a hand with a hole in the palm.

Huffing after Jack, Ben thought about slipping the spellcard into his Anvilsmith, but decided against it. If the card turned out to be a conjuration, Jack had enough distance on him that—if the creature came out tainted—there'd be only a fifty-fifty chance it would go after the intended target. It was just as likely to attack him as it was to go after Jack.

Turns in the stone hallway came quicker. Ben made another turn only to find they were in a long straightaway heading toward a door.

Desperately wanting to use his tablet to activate *Usain*, a speed spell he had renamed after Usain Bolt, to catch Jack, Ben knew if he stopped to cast, Jack would be through the door before the spell would activate.

Counter to his earlier thoughts, Ben wished the halls were longer.

Without losing a step, Jack clapped his hands and flashed purple again. When the light faded this time, he wore a new long black-haired wig, a long-tailed, gold lame server's coat, and a red kilt.

Jack went through the door.

Ben hit the door a bit later.

He busted into a kitchen. The full smell of baking bread and fried bacon smacked him. For a moment he forgot about the chase.

A little girl stood on a table skinning deer. Cast iron pots and pans bubbled and popped on two old-fashioned wood-burning stoves. Three men worked between the stoves and several large cauldrons over flames against a nearby wall, chopping carrots, peeling potatoes, and shucking corn.

All stopped in mid-motion. They looked from a swinging door—the way Jack must have gone—to Ben, and then to the girl.

A tomato from her direction grazed Ben's temple. She ordered in a not-so childlike voice, "Get out of my kitchen!"

Continuing after Jack, Ben swung the door open and scanned.

There were more than thirty men and women in the sitting room. All were older, with long gray hair and wore red and gold traditional-looking wizardly robes.

Large, comfortable chairs of varying width, height, and material filled the room. Each seat was unique, lavish, and high-backed with elaborate designs, arranged around old-fashioned, round wooden tables piled high with books, maps, and loose papers. Smaller personal round tables with food and drink flanked the chairs.

His eyes fell upon Jack.

On the opposite side of the room, the thief looked over his shoulder at Ben while moving around the last table toward another door.

Jack's outfit matched the server delivering a tray of drinks. The thief's throat tightened. He cried in a high, nasally voice—sounding exactly like a startled old woman, "Non-wizard. Non-wizard!"

No one looked to see where the voice came from.

They all focused on Ben.

Their eyes drank in his coat, short hair, and the peach fuzz threatening to sprout in uneven patches on his chin.

"Hold!" A woman two tables away commanded, her finger pointed at him.

Ben tried to move to call Jack out as a thief, but found himself frozen in place, unable to speak.

The man next to her stood and pointed. "Hold."

Three more *Hold* spells were cast on him in the following second.

Across the room, standing next to a mounted lion's head, Jack saluted with a snide smile. He exited through the opposite door which opened into a courtyard. The sound of horses trotting and an anvil being struck poured into the room.

"Bo!" The first woman called.

The door did not close after Jack went though.

A man, who had not pointed a finger, gotten up, or even looked away from the book in his lap smiled around the end of a pipe. His words came out in puffs of smoke. "If we caught him with a Hold spell, do you honestly believe we need Bo?" A soft laugh pressed more smoke out of his lungs as he turned the page and took another deep drag.

A hulking, furry minotaur ducked to clear his horns and twisted to squeeze his nine-foot tall, barrel-chested frame through the exterior door. Two sword hilts stuck out over a shoulder, extending as far beyond its body as its horns did. The door closed behind it.

Jack was gone.

The minotaur, Bo, headed at Ben in a single-minded fashion.

Ben wondered—if he hadn't been paralyzed—would he have ran away or messed his pants. The possibly of both wasn't out of the question.

After clearing a sword from its scabbard, the minotaur swung it back with both hands.

The blade looked longer than Ben was tall.

Fully torqued and ready to swing, Bo growled in a deep voice, "Whenever you're ready to release him."

Chapter Twelve

WHAT MAKES A WIZARD

THE AIR in Ben's nostrils weighed thick with fresh bread and bacon. Frozen by magic, he couldn't inhale or salivate. His stomach didn't grumble. The very real possibility of being cut in two by the massive minotaur didn't fill his body with fear or adrenaline.

He'd been reduced to nothing more than a cognizant statue.

They quarreled amongst themselves in a raspy, multisyllabic language that sounded like they'd taken Elven—a language he knew pretty well—and knocked the lofty way of speaking on its butt before dragging it for miles over glass and sandpaper.

When they looked at him, they didn't really seem to see him as a person. They'd look at his coat, his hair, his shoes, his pants, his tie, but never look him in the eyes.

Ben concentrated on being able to move.

The APA drilled on respecting elders, and if Master Reynolds were here, he'd probably be the youngest amongst this group. But they'd didn't acknowledge him, so why should he respect them?

He felt hunger begin to return. His stomach gurgled.

The only woman in all gold robes, the one who first hit him with a Hold spell, ears piqued. She turned from the people she talked to face him.

Warmth—power—chased hunger from his gut. Once his abdomen filled, the energy spread out through his body to push the paralysis away. As though lifting a great weight, sweat broke from Ben's brow as he struggled—and gained—control of his body. He exclaimed, "I am a wizard!"

Bo twitched.

Ben focused on controlling his sphincter.

The minotaur didn't swing.

Ben pointed at the door. "That server—"

"Ha!" The man with the pipe laughed smoke. He pulled a piece of paper from the table between them. Without raising his head, he presented it for Ben to see.

The paper had four large ornate red symbols on it. Ben didn't recognize any of them.

The man set the paper back on the table. "And you fancy yourself a wizard, hmm?"

Feeling his mouth tighten, Ben fought against clenching his teeth as he glared at the old man. "I *am* a wizard."

"Refer to yourself as a wizard again, boy," Bo growled slowly, his gaze remained set on Ben's neck. "And we will no longer be exchanging words."

The woman in all gold took a step forward. Her robes were exactly the same style as the ones in all the portraits. Her loose gray hair curled up slightly at the end to keep from sweeping the floor as she closed behind Bo and put her hand on the small of his massive back.

The minotaur untwisted and lowered his weapon.

"We," she motioned to include everyone in the room, but Ben and Bo, "my young Trencher, are wizards."

Knowing Jack would be long gone by now, Ben committed to the conversation. "I cast spells."

The man with the pipe, whose eyes were still in the book, chuckled. He spoke loudly to no one. "Anyone can get food from a full platter!"

Almost everyone nodded, smiled, chuckled, or did a combination of the three. Calm returned to the room.

Ben fumed. How could they just write him off like that?

"Dear," said the woman as she moved in front of Bo.

The Minotaur put his sword away.

She smiled in a grandmotherly way. "You may be able to cast spells, but you are far from being a wizard."

His fist tightened. He'd been learning about, and using, magic for six years.

Her next words made it obvious that she'd been reading his thoughts. "Yes, you surely are a Magic-User, a Trencher to be precise, but you are not yet, and may never become, a true Wizard."

Ben wanted to shake his head, but kept it still. What did she know? He could cast spells and he knew damn well what he was.

To negate his inner-affirmations, she added, "Yes, you do cast spells, but you are not a wizard. There is a line and, no—" She'd paused to acknowledge the rest of his thought that she was splitting hairs. "—the line is not that fine. To help, think about the difference between a wyrmling and a dragon."

Ben narrowed his eyes at her and tried to project, *Stop reading my thoughts.*

The old man with the pipe used a finger to bookmark the large tome in his lap. He removed his pipe. As though he were blind, his eyes drifted to the woman's back as he spoke. "He has potential."

They both looked at him, deep into his eyes.

He did his best not to think of anything so they couldn't start answering before he asked.

"True potential," she added.

"Agreed," the man said and went back to his pipe and book.

Motioning for Ben to walk with her as she went into the kitchen her armed with such fluidity that any liquid short of water would be jealous. "Come with me, dear. I will explain."

Chapter Thirteen

ARGOSIAN FONT

BEN TOOK in another deep inhalation. While he didn't know the name of the faint flowers, his lungs registered the freshest air he'd ever took in. Breathing on top of the Suntouched Spire made him feel silly for having ever visited an oxygen bar and paying for canned *Ocean Air*. Clear-headed, he felt honored to stand next to the woman, Elder Komir.

Though the sun shone on them, she'd raised her hands into the sky, and spoke in the raspy, warped Elven. She'd cast some spell that started to push the sun down and roll back the night.

Holy crap! Did she just cast a spell to move backward in time? He realized *honored* didn't do justice to how he felt, but he couldn't come up with a word better than *lucky*—and that didn't really fit either.

Three lamp-lit roads left the Suntouched Stronghold, the fort-city which expanded from the Spire. Elder Komir explained, *The road into the northern rolling hills leads to wild lands, where barbarians roam. The east road goes to that distant speck of light, which is Wilshire, this area's capitol.* She pointed to the last. *That one goes into a forest and, beyond that, an ocean.*

He knew he smelled salt water.

For a moment, Ben wondered how high they were, he wanted to go look over the edge, but felt his city-boy guts tighten each time he considered it.

Though she focused on where the roads went, Ben's eyes kept turning south.

Small blips of light moved as people moved backwards. Shorn crops mended as scythes and sickles worked away from the earth in a fast rewind fashion.

She had turned back time.

Astonished. That was the best word to describe the profound reverence he'd felt for her and her magic.

Deep shadowed forest, which hooked outward from the southeast all the way to the northwest, rose up to blot out the horizon. The trees at the northwest tip were the largest. Against them, at regular intervals, outpost lit as sunlight waned.

With the Stronghold arranged around the Spire, what did those distant stations guard against?

Night time again, Ben looked to the sky.

Clear. Totally clear. No smog. No light pollution. He spotted the North Star, the dippers, and a few other constellations. He regretted not committing more to memory than what was necessary to pass Astrology I & II. Still the stars were nearly the same as when he had seen them at Meadows Towing.

Elder Komir moved to stand in front of him. She projected softly, *We will get to that. For now, extend your arms.*

He did as she instructed. "Use words please."

If you want me out... She slid a bracelet onto his left wrist, her thoughts became stern like he imagined her words would have been, *...you have to will me out.* She slid a second bracelet onto his right.

"How do I—" Ben stopped. Caught by a swell of energy, his head lulled back. Another wave traveled from his feet, through his torso, and down his arms to rhythmically pulse in his hands. It—magic—throbbed gentler than the hard whacking feeling from using a tablet. Instead of the energy being forced into his being, the magic came from within his chest.

He checked the seeping feeling around his hands. They radiated with Argosian red.

Ben steeled his thoughts to try and keep her out.

Good. She transmitted, *I can no longer read you, but I am still able to send.* She smiled. *Shielding is a step on the path to blocking, and infinitely more vital.*

Between casting the black-eagle fiend, The Painting, and Kograkken's ominous farewell, Ben didn't want her to sense his relief at seeing crimson energy surrounding his hands instead of black.

Elder Komir pointed to his hands. *This is magic, but not magic as you know it.* She pulled one of the lockets from around her neck. *For saving my great-granddaughter, you will know true magic.* She placed the thin necklace on him.

Another energy swell.

He nearly swooned.

The warmth of its vibration gathered and rolled in his chest.

This magic is not channeled by a device, as you are

*doubtlessly accustomed.** She pressed a hand to his chest over the locket.

Like a clog had been removed, magic coursed through his heart, veins, and arteries. Every hair on his body felt like a lightning rod, diverting ambient energy from the air into him.

His blood began to feel like raw energy.

Letting it wash through him, wanting the euphoria to never end, his eyes rolled and closed. "Yes," escaped his lips.

She removed her hand, and the magic kept swimming through his veins. *This is close to what it feels like to be a wizard.**

Ben nodded. His body swayed with the rhythm pulsing through him. "How do I become a true wizard?"

*Study and practice. And plenty of both.** She showed him his remaining spellcard and placed it in his hand. *You do not know any proper spells yet, but until you do, the energy you feel can be channeled through these.**

"But it's cursed."

*Pish-posh!** She sent, and he felt the air around him react as she waved her hand in three quick, dismissive arcs. *When you are a wizard, the only curses that stick are those in which you believe.** She looked at his spellcard hand. *Focus the energy into your spell-square.**

Fearing the worst, he warned, "Be ready," Ben pushed a small amount of his energy into his SD card. A conjured swarm of red bees sprung from his hands. The swarm gathered above him and waited for commands. He didn't have to take the reins. The conjurer's link had formed automatically, and he was already in control.

Normally the spellcard would have been destroyed. He'd then have to catch the data strip, scavenge what he could from the remains, and return home to build a new circuit board and housing. Amazed, he held the card, which looked as though it hadn't even been used.

Cast again, she urged.

Ben summoned four more swarms before the energy, which had become a part of him, faded. The spellcard never broke apart.

The large, buzzing mass of five crimson swarms was indistinguishable to the eye. Yet, he could feel each individual casting. He used them to form *B E N* in red buzzing letters.

You have used all of the universal energy available to you before resting. Elder Komir beamed at him and took a step back. Obviously, she expected big things from him. *Now, tap into your personal energies and let the true magic happen.*

Ben focused on channeling his own energy into the spellcard. An extra energy swell rolled in the center of his mind.

The energy felt anxious to be released.

A freezing shiver ran through him. An ice-cold pang racked his brain. He dropped the card and turned away from Elder Komir to look at the black energy around his hands.

The magic from his brain tried to force its way out to get into the spellcard. *Use me.* The Nilosian energy surrounded his hands pulsed.

Stumbling away from her, he tried to will it back in.

Elder Komir screamed to him.

Ben couldn't make sense of her words. He felt dizzy. Scared. Exhausted. Angry.

A fog, with a fury of its own rolled in his head. *It* desperately wanted to be used.

A strange sensation—falling—filled him before he blacked out.

BEN WOKE. No idea where he was, he floated in blackness with no sense of direction. Did he face north? East? Down?

He wasn't alone.

A voice, sounding like his own, but malicious and all too close, whispered, "The first person we should kill is Collins."

Ben recalled the Senior Adept patting him down. As though outside his body, he could see the blond Adept switch his Anvilsmith with the one in the booth. Not wanting to, Ben couldn't help but agree, "It's his fault."

"Exactly." The voice. "He did this to us."

Ben could feel a small but potent rage at his core. He questioned it. "Us?"

The dark rage—the frenzied wrath—rushed to fill him. "Us!"

BEN SPRANG FROM THE BED. Blankets entangled his legs. He tripped and fell to the fur-covered floor.

Penelope, in long crimson robes, leapt onto the chair

she'd been sitting on. Her hands were extended, ready to cast.

He lay on the fur rug, breathing hard, looking up at a red-marbled ceiling. The fall had awoken the many aches from Kograkken's backhand.

She asked, "*Us* what?"

"Huh?" Realizing he wasn't alone, Ben imagined his brain behind four layers of steel.

Penelope answered, "You screamed, '*Us*.'"

Ben rubbed his face as he tried to steady his breathing. He didn't want to answer that question. Heck, he didn't know *how* to answer. He shrugged and remembered his stolen spellcards. Guessing the likely answer, he asked anyway. "Where's Jack?"

She asked, "Who?"

Warm against him, Elder Komir's locket slid across his bare chest when Ben rolled onto his side to look at Penelope. Argosian energy softly pulsed in his chest. A different energy—the Nilosian energy—boiled in his mind. He couldn't focus on anything but Jack.

The dark magic wanted to be tapped, and lusted to inflict exacting vengeance upon the thief.

Worse yet, Ben did, too.

Chapter Fourteen

PRINCIPLE

EACH STAGE of their four course lunch had been orchestrated by a foppish servant in golden silk robes. A league of servants in red silken robes carted the old food away and brought new.

Not interested in food, Ben had barely managed to eat a handful of grapes and strawberries. Both Elder Komir and Penelope told him to put the theft of his spellcards out of his mind, but how could he? If it were only that easy.

A slight stinging, like a low-grade headache forming, seemed to taint Ben's thoughts.

While Elder Komir picked from platters overflowing with juicy meat and dozens of different cheeses, she had tried to comfort Ben by pointing out that the loss of his spellcards had ferreted out the spy within the Suntouched Spire. As a reward for his loss, besides an unspendable *thank you*, she'd also given him a thick—useless—dusty book with weird symbols in it to study until he could get back through Pepperjacks.

Unspendable? What kind of jerk-thought was that? It didn't feel like his own.

Ben had wanted to pinch himself. That wasn't his way of thinking at all. If Elder Komir offered the book, it must have value. Heck, even if it didn't, she'd given him the gift of being able to cast without technology. True magic. He had no idea how long it'd be before he was a real wizard, but now he at least felt his feet were on the path.

That stinging in his head painted Penelope, too. It was as though she had been no better than her great-grandmother when she had agreed and given him a small pouch of coins. She admitted her family owned Pepperjacks and promised management there would more than reimburse him for his stolen items. He'd only have to give the purse to any Pepperjacks employee.

While Ben had considered the stinging a word—*Us* —pulsed in his head. Remembering the darkness of the dream, Ben tried to lock the ingratitude and *Us* away in a steel box as the Komirs tried to console him... but the stinging had continued.

The old guy with the pipe came, had sat at the table with a book, and didn't said a word. He flipped a page, took a puff, and mumble into his beard.

Ben had spent half a school year crafting each one of those cards. Jack hadn't merely helped himself to seven easily replaced or forgotten SD spellcards, he had stolen three-and-a-half years of Ben's blood, sweat, and magic.

None of them understood, though. How could they? They weren't technomancers like—*Us*—him.

It was easy for them to tell him to just let it go. The massive meal, just for the four to them, had told the tale of them never having to skimp or scratch or claw to earn enough to buy supplies for school projects. They had tossed him a few token gifts and expected him to forget the theft.

He couldn't. He wouldn't.

The man with the pipe said Jack would've headed to the docks for a quick escape...

...And that was where Ben went after ditching the guard keeping tabs on him. He had hopped on a wagon heading to the docks and kept his eyes peeled for Jack.

Now, Ben sat at the docks. He'd been for half the day. The rolling sapphire water gently lapping against the bay threatened to steal his anger as he watched the ebb and flow of waves. Similarly, ships came in, did their business, and left.

"Are you lost, long hair?" A rough-talking man stood in front of Ben. A wide Captain's hat on his head, grizzled gray hair covered his chin. A telescope hung from one hip next to a rapier, and, on the opposite hip, a dagger. Faded brown leather leggings tucked into knee-high boots and his loose cloth shirt billowed from the eastward breeze.

Ben turned his gaze to the docks. Quietly comparing this guy's dress to the folks there. All of them appeared fresh from being extras on a *Pirates of the Caribbean* movie. Add eyeliner, a pistol, and a bottle of rum and this guy could be Captain Jack's father.

Best to ignore him.

Undaunted, the man continued, "If'n you're lookin'

to get lost, I've got the best ship on the seas to do it with." The man motioned vaguely further down the docks to where three ships were being unloaded.

Unsure which one he should be appraising, Ben eyed each. They were large and sleek. He didn't know anything about boats, but they looked faster than the massive blocky ships he had seen earlier.

"Five Stags will get you clear to First Light." The Captain let a boisterous laugh loose to cover up checking over his shoulders. He then whispered, "And ten will keep it secret *if'n* you really want to go."

Ben shook his head and took a moment to fix his mind to imitate the pompous Komir accent like he'd heard in the Suntouched Spire. "No, I do not want to broker passage. I am looking for someone." Unrolling a length of cloth he had drawn the pattern of Jack's back tattoo on, Ben showed it to the sailor. "He has body markings in this shape."

Looking around the dock again, the man leaned in. "If'n I was you, I'd be careful with showin' that around." He folded the cloth over twice, his calloused hands closing Ben's own hand around it. "The Friendships don't much care for people who're lookin' for one of their members."

"Friendships?" Ben asked.

The man muttered, "Long hairs..." He looked around the docks again. He spoke in a loud, patronizing tone, "Where is your guard?"

A set of whistles sounded. Dockworkers. Being there for half the day, Ben already knew what the main whistles meant. Laborers from one ship exited the now-empty vessel and doubled up to work the next boat.

Over his shoulder, Ben only found dockworkers and seamen, he had lost the knight who tried to trail him at a distance. "Don't have one."

Leaning away from Ben, the Captain looked him over, his eyes focusing on the long, red robes and the wig—pulled from Jack's scalp—on Ben's head. He stepped closer and rested his forearms on his raised knee. His voice lowered again. "You mean to tell me you left the Red Spike without swords at your call?"

Ben took a deep breath of the salty air and tightened his grip on his last SD card. He'd reprogrammed it from the swarm's specifications to Orion's and had included the scrapyard combat data. Deep in his palm, he prepped to channel magic into it. "Don't need them."

"You've got spirit, boy!" The Captain pulled away and let loose another boisterous laugh.

Not feeling it, Ben smiled with him.

The man added, "And a heapin' extra helping of dumb."

Ben's smile waned.

The Captain chuckled, "If'n your purse went to a cutthroat, it'd be a shame." He pointed to one of the many sea worn brick-walled taverns. "Buy me lunch, boy, and I'll tell you what I know for a Stag."

"My name is Ben."

The Captain smiled at him. "Quite demandin', aren't we?" He then continued without moving his lips. The rasp and broken words disappeared. "While I am saving your life, long hair, you are going to go by *Boy* and you will call me Captain. Got it?"

Ben blinked at the sudden change. Then nodded.

Chapter Fifteen

THE EVEN KEEL

THE STENCH OF ALCOHOL, sweat, and mildew hung in the Even Keel's air. Ben and Captain made their way through six long tables to one of the two booths in the back. Captain eased his way down, and Ben fell into the seat expecting it to offer resistance, but his teeth clacked. The cushion had long lost its spring.

Captain drummed his fingers on the table. "The Stag?"

Ben reached into the small bag—which he refused to call a purse—and pulled out a few of the steel pieces under the table. Comparing them, he separated a coin with a Stag's bust on both sides from similar Sun-embossed ones. Sliding the rest back in, Ben put his hand face down on the table, covering the coin, and prompted, "The Friendships?"

Captain smiled, he extended his hand to be next to Ben's. "The coin."

Ben's hand had barely left the coin.

Captain covered it and kept eye contact with Ben's

while he pulled it back with a slight scrape. His eyes flicked to the coin cradled in his lap for a second. "It's open talk for The Guilds, or The Brotherhoods, or whatever else the collective thieves' dens deem fancy enough to refer to their *profession* as a whole."

A server came with a dented, oblong platter piled high with different slices of meats and roasted red potatoes. She filled out all the curves of her stained, flowing light gray dress. Pressing her chest against Captain's back, she set the food in front of him with a peck on his grizzled cheek. "There you go, Cornelius."

Ben's eyes rose from her low-cut blouse.

With a wink, she turned her lustful smile on him.

Caught, Ben's cheeks burned.

She asked, "Anything for your new cabin boy?"

"He ain't—" Cornelius—Captain—popped a potato into his mouth, and steam puffed out between open-mouthed chomps. "—earned his salt just yet."

"Shame." She licked her lips and twirled away.

Ben's shin lit with pain and he bounced in his seat. Cornelius had kicked him. He stopped watching the server's swaying hips to frown at the man.

Cornelius spoke without moving his lips again. "She'd be the first to slit you." He speared a slice of meat with a knife, brought it to his mouth, and spoke before taking a bite. "With how anxious you are, Boy, you'd probably not even get your relief first."

Ben shook his head. He wondered if Cornelius knew the difference between taking *in* beauty and being taken *by* beauty. His mind flashed back to Penelope running in the hallway. Ben shook the memory away. "So, to which Friendship does the guy I'm looking for belong?"

"From the looks of it," Cornelius spoke through a disappearing mouthful of meat. "You've got yourself a Brother of the Bottomless Palm." He paused to add a quarter of potato to his mouth which helped to quiet the smacking. "Ask anyone who knows of them and they'll agree, The Palm are the greediest of the lot. Also, the most daring."

"Greed and daring." Ben recalled how Jack's eyes had focused on his Anvilsmith and spellcards before befriending him.

"Aye, deadly combo. No other guild would dare to infiltrate the Red Spike, but, if the money is right, The Palm will try anything." Cornelius speared a potato Ben had been eyeing and offered it.

Ben took it and bobbled it hand-to-hand to cool. "Where can I find them?"

"Keep flashing that drawing and you won't." Cornelius stopped and turned an ear.

Ben listened to the whistles with him.

Cornelius grinned. "The dockworkers have finished my boat."

Having heard the finishing sound a dozen times, Ben nodded.

Cornelius said, "Soon, they'll all be in here swallowing swill until the next boat comes." He pointed to Ben's robes and hair. "It will serve you well to lose the robes and hide the hair. They might show your status up at the Red Spike and Red Brick, but out here, they'll get you cut."

Ben repeated his question, "Where can I find them?"

"Are you listening to me, Boy?" Cornelius pointed the knife at him. "I'm saying like that..." He jabbed with the knife at the air pointing to Ben's robes and hair. "You won't. They'll find you, cut you, and walk away richer." He waved his knife around his face and hat. "You die seeing me last, and the Red Spike will have my head for sure."

Ben kept from balling his fists, but his frustration sounded in his wavering voice. "Then what do I do?"

Cornelius motioned to the server who, not having anyone else to serve, whirled back to the table. "I need some proper local color for my boy here. Those worked for smuggling him from Lomka, but now I need to get him up to the Ros'."

Her attention solely on Cornelius, she turned her back on Ben to face the Captain. "In exchange for those red silks, I'm sure I can find somethin' that'll keep the Dock Master from waking up."

"Good." Cornelius took a small bite of meat. "Keep him sleepin'."

Ben bit into the potato, looked away from their flirting, and out the window. Not jealous of the workers' labor, he eyed them as they teemed like ants on the remaining ship. The delicious mixture of garlic and other seasoning brought his attention back to the potato.

On the edge of his vision, Ben spied a note extended behind the server to him. He reached for it, but missed when Cornelius sent her away with a hearty smack on her rear.

Cornelius stood. "She's going to try and undress you. Don't let her." He then slid the platter, and what remained of the meal, across to Ben. "Once you're changed, and fit in with this lot, I'll send you the information."

About to leave, Ben grabbed the man's wrist.

Cornelius barely turned his head, looking down at Ben's hand on him. His voice, a sharp blade. "Boy?"

Ben snaked his hand back. He clasped it in his lap. "Why not just tell me now?"

"Because, seeing how thick you are, you'd probably go right away." He looked Ben up and down one more time. "And if you are truly from the Suntouched Stronghold, no less the Spire, your eyes need time to forget my face."

As the Captain walked away, Ben discovered a note under the plate.

Chapter Sixteen

LOOKING THE PART

THE SERVER HAD COME BACK with a bundle of clothes. She tried to make Ben give up the red robes first, but heeding Cornelius' warning, he demanded the clothes instead. He slipped behind the booth to change and found a note in the pocket, *Salt or not, for two silvers we can share the night. Cornelius need not be the wiser.*

Ben removed the wig.

A muffled sigh came from a dark hole in the dark wood. She must've been watching him from a secret area.

He turned his back to where he heard the sound come from. Ben pulled on the loose tan V-neck cotton top and brown cotton pants. It almost felt like wearing the old-fashioned pajamas his grandmother had given him.

Holding his tablet, he faked a trip and jammed his tablet between the booth and the wall.

As though nothing had happened, Ben then slipped the red cotton sash through the wide pant loops. There wasn't enough to go around twice. The excess hung from the knot he tied. Now, except for his haircut, he looked like he belonged amongst the pirate extras.

"Best to be rid of those fine shoes and into one of the pairs there." Her voice mostly carried over the booth, but also slipped from her viewing station.

Ben grimaced at the repulsive hodgepodge of worn leather boots, tattered cloth shoes, and frayed rope sandals. No telling who wore them last or what nastiness waited to spread.

From habit, Ben pulled the loose cloth together around his neck to fasten a top button that wasn't there. Suddenly worried about cleanliness, he sniffed at the collars. Only finding the salty scent of the sea, he let them fall open.

Keeping his red leather boots on, he stepped out.

Hip kicked out to the side, top a little wider exposing a bit more cleavage than before, she waited.

Trying to be polite, he handed over the robes, the wig, and cleared his throat before handing over the note with a soft. "No, thank you."

She accepted all the items, but the wig captured her attention as she turned and left.

Ben returned to the booth. He slipped the Captain's note out again—*codeword cheeks*—and put it away. What was that about?

Another set of whistles sounded the arrival of a fourth ship. Ben's last potato had gone cold before the third and fourth ships were both unloaded.

As Cornelius had predicted, workers brought in a fresh wave of sweat for the cushions, ordered, dropped copper and silvers coins, and drank ale by the pitchers.

A bartender had come in and help the server keep up with business.

Just as the crews worked on the ships, they worked in the building. Lively whoops, hoots, and hollers shook the structure when a three-piece band—two mandolins and a drummer—started rounds of bawdy drinking songs.

As though timed to an inaudible cue, the workers stopped their revelry. A few took bread, but other food and drink where left where they lay as the workers piled down to the docks.

Ben's eyebrows raised. When did the new ship pull in? How had they heard it?

After cleaning up most of the mugs and leaving platters with food, the server returned with a heel of bread for him.

Ben spun the empty platter, muttering Cornelius's *fit in* sentence. How in the heck was he supposed to do that?

She leaned in to take the platter. Though she got close, she avoided pressing her body against his. The small smile she showed him felt genuine. "If you want to fit in, learn the songs or—" Her elbow kicked out to the docks. "—go work with them."

Ben shook his head and tried to button the non-existent collar button again. "I don't know how to do that kind of labor."

"No one does the first time." She gave him a wink. "Just get out there. They'll show you the ropes."

Chapter Seventeen

ONE OF US

WHILE WORKING ON SHIPS, Ben slid away and hid whenever he spied men and women wearing red leather armor with golden studs walking by. On their torsos, they wore a badge he'd seen inside the Suntouched Stronghold. It had a red spire, outlined in yellow, which stood in front of a red sun, also outlined in the same yellow. It was the same armor as the guard who he had ditched.

They combed the docks, but didn't board.

He had reacted to seeing them the first time and bumped into a bald, tattooed man who reeked of cloves.

He nodded to Ben.

Ben nodded back.

A quick shrill whistle sounded twice each time the guards came around, and they came around often. Each time he'd drop out of sight and would see someone else hiding.

They'd nod to each other.

Soon, all the crates were emptied and new cargo loaded. Ben returned to the Even Keel with the dockworkers.

Oddly enough, the funky mildew scent had disappeared. All he smelled upon re-entering was seasoned meat and garlic potatoes. His arms, back, and legs ached, but the soreness amplified his want of the well-seasoned food.

The man who had repeatedly blown the warning whistle raised his drink. "Cups up."

Everyone grabbed one of the earlier abandoned mugs. Anyone empty handed raised a fist. Ben followed the latter group's their example.

The whistler raised his chin. "Those Redblades were hungry today, boys, but we all remained free!" He shook his flagon and liquid splashed over. Unrestrained cheers sounded through the room before the spilt drink hit the table. "Drinks down!"

Having drained his cup, the man wiped his mouth dry with the back of his arm and called, "Music!"

The trio got up and played.

Ben learned and yelled the lewd lyrics right along with the rest. As with the others who were younger, he'd been given a wooden cup of water in place of ale. The worker part of him wanted to try the brown drink, and he almost swiped a mug before he remembered why he had worked in the first place.

He'd been accepted as one of them.

Seeing some of the other younger workers trying to sneak a drink, Ben made a purposefully slow attempt at a mug.

"Na'uh." The bald, clovey tattooed man lifted it out of his reach with a knowing smile.

A boy no older than ten, the same age as Ben had been when he became an Initiate for his first eighth at the Archon Private Academy, tried as well. The kid managed to drain one before catching a heavy boot in the butt for it.

The whistler called, "Wood boys out!"

This ban on youth applied to everyone underage. Anyone drinking from a wooden cup—five, Ben included—had to leave.

On their way out, the whistler pushed an almost perfectly halved silver coin with a raised lion's head on both sides in each boy's hand.

The sun had gone down and cool air washed in from the sea.

They stood in the street. The five of them, each holding their wage.

The ten-year-old's words came out slurred. "Let's go to the Beakless Griffon." He pointed vaguely. "They'll let anyone with coin drink until they pass out there."

Ben cheered with the others. For a moment, he considered returning to the Even Keel and wait outside for Cornelius.

Just then, another boy, Ben's height, slung his arm around his shoulder and started singing.

Ben smiled and sang with him. The others joined in as they made their way down the wharf and, near the end, turned away from the witnesses on the docks.

Chapter Eighteen

THE BEAKLESS GRIFFIN

ALONE, as though sent away from the other taverns as punishment, a squat, two-story structure sunk into the earth. Its horribly cracked deep blue paint exposed a gray layer, and under where the gray peeled away, light blue. Even at a distance, music poured from inside. A piano played the loudest.

The song inside floated their way. *Boomerang Jane.* They'd sung it at the Even Keel. The song about a quiet dock master's daughter becoming a pirate captain struck a chord with Ben. If she knew what she'd develop into, would she still had made the same choices?

Ben led the group in changing tunes.

Walking down the slope to the front door, Ben noted the griffon-shaped wooden sign swaying in the wind. Indistinguishably faint divots, carved letter or symbols had long since faded and been painted over. Plain wood shone where the mythical animal's beak would have had been worn smooth with time.

When the first of his group opened the door, a roared greeting rolled out of the building. The smell of alcohol within overpowered the salty sea behind them. The muggy warmth from below collected on Ben's skin and a soft crosswind licked his dampening hair.

Halfway down the slope, Ben paused at the top of the short set of stairs.

For a reason he couldn't quite nail down, this felt like the point of no return that Boomerang Jane had faced. Ben nodded to set his resolve and descended into the growing heat and noise. Ready to take in the rowdy madness, he crossed the threshold.

"Coin!" A voice bellowed from his right.

Ben jumped.

A wide mouth of golden teeth barked laughter. The man who'd startled him hooted, slapped his knee, and pointed at Ben. "Got cha!"

Working a smile to his face, Ben handed the gold-toothed joker his half-silver.

The man turned the coin over in his hand, dipped it in an amber fluid, and watched in. His gold teeth flashed as he spoke, but the ruckus proved too much to overcome.

Not wanting to, Ben leaned toward the man. "What?"

The man gave a sly wink. "You want leaks, weeks, or beaks?"

About to yell a question about the difference, Ben remembered the Captain's note. "Cheeks."

Gold-teeth nodded as though he'd expected nothing less. He set the half-coin over a slit on a tiny wooden table. With the press of a button, a blade shot down, and cut the coin into two quarters. The man held one of the quarters toward Ben with that. same sly wink. "Cheeks it is then, brother."

Ben accepted the sliver and returned the wink.

Gold-teeth swept three half coins and two quarters into a small wicker basket. He hung the basket on rusty hook connected to a length of rope. The bucket began to rise.

Scanning to where the bucket would go, a smiling, red-haired man with an air of authority looked down at Ben. Fat rubies lined the golden goblet in his hand. The guy looked familiar. From the docks? Having made eye contact, the man raised his cup in greeting and nodded.

Ben nodded back.

Next to the redhead, another man pulled the rope. With brown hair chopped short in a haphazard fashion, his face held a permanent scowl. Deeper on the left, scars ran up both cheeks. He didn't wear a patch to cover the wrecked and sunken eyelid over the shadowed socket.

With a shudder, Ben turned his eyes away. He found the beat with the seven-piece band and sang along, "No, Jane. You'll surely hang if you dare to cross your father again."

In three evenly-spaced rows from the stage, eighteen long tables divided the main floor. They were bolted down and, somehow, twice as packed as the full tables at the Even Keel. The boys he'd come in with had scattered through the building. Only the smallest, the one that had gotten them kicked out, could be found— and only by the narrow gap he made amongst the rambunctious patrons.

The tables nearly butted against four booths lined up on the back wall. All taken. In the booth furthest to the right, sat Cornelius, his hat pulled low to cover his face.

Seven shapely women in vibrant light blue dresses, nearly fluorescent from the many glass-contained light orbs bouncing in a fancy chandelier, made their way into the room. The vivacious women served, cleaned, danced, and sang.

Ben lost the words to Boomerang Jane...

He picked up the tune again. "No, Jane. You've got nothing to gain, why dare cross your father again?"

A second floor overlooked the first, and at least fifty men and women filled the visible areas of space, but there were no stairs or ropes leading up. Trying to piece it together, Ben wondered how one gets up there? Their faces were stern and set. Like gargoyles. The man with the goblet seemed to be the only one capable of smiling.

Some of them were focused on Ben.

He squeezed into a nearby table and looked for utensils. None. Everyone pulled portions with their dirty hands—some with gloves, most without—before plopping meat or cheese into their mouths.

The stares from the second floor felt like a weight on his shoulders. Now wasn't the time to be squeamish. Ben picked a strip of greasy warm meat with his bare hands. Under the slick feel, the meat felt tough. He put it in his mouth to pull a bite away. Tasty juice oozed into his mouth, but his teeth verified the lack of tenderizing. He placed the full piece in his mouth and worked at it.

Three styles of wooden cups to grab filled the spaces

between platters. The drunk kid—a natural born lush—from the Even Keel grabbed the smallest style. *It must have the highest alcohol content.* Factoring that in, Ben took the tallest of the three types.

He brought it to his mouth and smelled cherries. A sip confirmed the strongest ingredient of the red drink along with a faint hint of roasted almonds which faded to a slightly bitter aftertaste.

The weight of stares began to lift.

Still not daring to inspect the second floor again, Ben noticed Cornelius' hat at a normal angle. He made eating motions with his hands.

Ben set the cup down and dove for the last heel of bread before one of the lovely servers danced away with the nearly empty platter.

She winked at him.

Not sure if the Captain would approve, he smiled secretly and bit into the deliciously buttered honey oat. This was the kind of bread his mother liked to make. The grain felt heartier than anything she'd made and Ben liked it. He wanted more. More of all of it.

Chapter Nineteen

DEN OF THIEVES

A GONG RANG from the second floor. The music stopped and the din started to die. The gong rang again. The red-haired man with the ruby encrusted gold goblet raised it over the edge. "Cups up, lads. Cups up."

Ben joined everyone in lifting a cup.

"Last night started what could be the end for the Red Spike, and word has come…" He flicked the chalice. It gave a dull thunk. "Even Leighlan Komir, the *Red Baron* himself, had to join in the fray."

Everyone cheered.

To blend, Ben cheered with them. He liked Elder Komir. He hadn't met Leighlan the Red Baron, but something about the way the redhead talked about him made Ben's neck hairs stiffen.

The man continued, "Granted, we make our money anywhere we can…" he paused, and everyone shared a dirty laugh. "We all know there is money in war, and of all the casters, the Argosians are notoriously cheap!"

A mixture of chiding laughs and hardy boos fill the room.

Ben added to both in turn.

"So," the man raised his goblet higher, his smile broadening as he swirled the cup. "This cups up is for whichever force takes down the Red—"

"Guild Master," the young boy slurred. His shrill voice cut through the room. Everyone looked at him. "What if Orange comes in, or worse, White?"

"Use your brain, Meacon." All eyes returned to the man and his broad smile. "Do you really think either of them wants to war with Red?" He shook his head. "No, as long as a deeper color doesn't control The Node, they're happy holdin' hands and singing songs!" He crossed his eyes and bobbled his head.

The band struck up a jaunty tune. Their piper punctuated the highs with happy pipe bursts. The rest of the band came to a sudden stop, but the piper kept chirping away. Copying the Guild Master, his eyes were crossed and he bobbled his head. When two of the other band members mock-stabbed the piper, cheers rang out. The piper's toots worsened and weakened with each fake stab in his fake death.

"Brother!" Cornelius called out. All heads looked to him as he tilted his hat back to see the second floor. "Do you foresee success?"

The man looked into his goblet. His smile died and a somber expression washed over his face. "One can never know for certain."

Ben noticed an oracular glint to the man's eyes. He seemed to be looking through the cup.

"If the Argosians are able to keep a grip on victory's

hips, we'll serve them as well." He seemed to come back into himself and took a small sip. Losing the fight to keep the smile from his face as he spoke over the rim. "Though my glass wouldn't be as full!"

Cheers arose, and his grin flashed back to full force.

The man addressed Cornelius, "Worry not, my good Captain. From what I hear, your native land has the upper hand."

Cornelius raised his cup, one of the smaller ones, and bowed his head.

Breaking the dying cheer, Meacon spoke, his voice higher than before and his words slushier. "I heard they got the girl back!"

Everyone seemed annoyed with him. Ben wanted to help Meacon keep quiet, but there were too many bodies between them.

Searching the room, the Guild Master purposefully avoided eye contact with the servers in light blue as he pointed at Meacon. "Someone get that boy another drink!"

Soft laughter arose as someone near Meacon put one of the small cups in his small hands.

The man added, "True, Penelope is back, but she'll be of no help tonight and she doesn't have the key!"

This last statement lost the general populous.

Ben did not know how to react.

The servers, band members, and bartender clapped. Finally showing life, everyone on the second floor joined in.

Those at the tables searched one another with weak, wanting smiles.

The man raised his goblet to those on the second

floor and spoke flatly to the main floor. "This is a good thing."

Everyone cheered again, and Ben joined.

"So, everyone. Cups up!" He paused, looking over everyone in the room. Making sure no one had want for a cup, he commanded with a sharp nod, "Drinks down!"

The only ones who really slammed their drinks back were the one with the smaller cups. Those with medium and large cups took a swig.

Ben raised the cup to his lips and his eyes went back to Cornelius for direction.

Suddenly the Captain jabbed an angry finger at him. "Boy!"

Ben froze. The drink wetting his upper lip.

Everyone stared at him.

He lowered his cup. "Yes, Captain?"

"Are my quarters clean?" Cornelius shot out of the booth, taking long thumping strides toward Ben.

Everyone shifted, pressing against others, to give Cornelius a clear path.

Not knowing how to answer. Ben tensed. "Yes."

Cornelius grabbed him by the scruff of the neck and shook hard. "I thought I saw you doing dock work today."

"True." A gruff voice called. "He was there, Cap."

Ben tried to look, but Cornelius had a tight grip on him.

A woman's voice rang out. "I saw him there too, Cap."

Ben opened his mouth to reply, but Cornelius dragged him toward the door and yelled over him,

"You're saying you're fast enough to clean *and* do side work *and* drink?"

Doing his best to not fight the strong hand gripping him, Ben went with Cornelius.

Roars of laughter and insults followed them across the room and out the door. Most encouraged Cornelius to give him—the scrub—a solid beating. The scarred, eye-less man from the second floor growled. "Run sweet-meat across the deck 'til the edge is gone from those pretty red lady-boots."

"Tell me the order in which you cleaned, boy!" Up the stairs, the slope, and a few paces away from the building, Cornelius still held Ben in tight control. He began to speak in a low, angry voice.

Ben tried to follow the low words, but lost them when Cornelius sent a telepathic message. *My informant just relayed the news. The Palm's spy is returning to the Suntouched Spire to assure none loyal to Red can join in defending The Node.* He turned Ben around when they hit the sand. His mouth still moved with whispers.

Ben ignored the words and focused on the voice in his head.

Cornelius projected, *You have to warn Elder Komir.*

Ben's mouth opened to ask who was the spy and closed it to rephrase the question.

You know him. Cornelius had read his mind. *He probably still has your spellcards since they haven't hit the black market yet.*

Ben pressed his lips together and narrowed his eyes at the Captain in suspicion.

Cornelius' face morphed, changing to the knight who had trailed him for the first half of the day. The features shifted, and the guard's skin paled to match Elder Komir's wizard-friend, the one with the book and pipe. Then the features slacked, darkened, and contracted back to Cornelius's face. *Understand?*

Ben nodded.

Cornelius got loud again and gave Ben two more shakes before turning him back to the boats. The Captain slipped Ben's Anvilsmith down the front of his shirt.

About to ask how Cornelius got it, a swift kick lit on Ben's butt. He ran.

The Captain yelled after him, "The galley better be spotless! You hear me, boy? Spotless!"

Chapter Twenty

SUNTOUCHED SHOWDOWN

Just after sundown, Ben made it back to the Suntouched Stronghold from the docks. As much as he wanted to rush in, he took the time to help the elderly wagoner—who'd kindly gave him a free ride—stable the horses.

Ben had gotten used to the animals' smell on the road, but a stable full of them, their feed, and their waste, proved to be an aromatic nightmare.

Someone slowly whistled the filthy *Heave Your Load* song. A song that made Ben blush in the Even Keel once he understood the lyrics. The tune, when drawn-out in a lazy dawdle, almost sounded like a love song.

Ben bent to see the whistler from under the horse.

Coming from the long clearing to the red marbled spire, a man—about Jack's height, Jack's slender build —in red robes and with his hood pulled up, looked around casually as he strolled toward the stables.

Ben pulled his tablet and last spellcard from the

wagon. At the doors of the stable, Ben called to the whistler. "Hey, Jack."

The person, who may not have been Jack, didn't even glance. He pivoted and sprinted back toward the spire.

Ben channeled Argosian energy into the spell card. "Jack!" The snapping energy flew into his fist. The distance at which he could cast Orion had grown. The faint red shadowy gorilla formed next to him before Orion's actual body materialized. Instead of taking control, Ben pointed at Jack. "Stop him!"

Orion thumped after the fleeing thief.

Ben leapt the chain barring wagons and followed. If Jack got into the spire, it'd be over.

Orion lunged.

Jack rolled to the side.

Ben's conjuration blew past, rolled, and turned.

A fully materialized gorilla, made of purple energy, sprang from Jack's hands.

Ben's mouth fell open. He blinked in disbelief. No one had ever summoned a creature with such rapidity.

On the ground, Jack flashed a defiant smile. "Don't know how you survived the room of wizards last night, but I hope you're ready?"

Their gorillas faced each other.

Jack's eyes became glassy—the look of someone inhabiting his conjuration.

Ben slid his consciousness into Orion as the gorillas charged and clashed.

On initial impact, Jack's gorilla pushed Orion back.

Orion caught the purple fists on the down stroke. Snagging the control reins, Ben gripped them, pushed

Orion's hips into the gorilla, and twisted while pulling. The purple gorilla flipped over them from the hip throw. Ben released.

Orion leapt to rain his fists down on the fallen foe.

The purple gorilla caught Orion's wrists and pressed to get back to its feet.

Standing, Orion leaned his weight in, but Jack's gorilla managed to get a foot under and made slow progress in standing.

Ben backed into his own body. This shouldn't be happening. He had rarely activated the actual spellcard Jack used. His own SD had easily been through a hundred use cycles. Orion should've been dominating this contest.

Yet, the purple gorilla was somehow stronger and had gotten to its feet.

Ben pulled his Anvilsmith and cued up *Heracles*, his strength spell. Not meaning to, he gawked at the power meter. How was it full? It had been at nine last night and only gained an *awatt* per hour, as nearly all devices did. It should've been at thirty-three.

A frustrated grunt brought Ben's attention back.

Jack's gorilla not only had its feet beneath it, it towered over Orion, forcing him down to a knee.

Ben tapped *Cast*.

Though not visible against the evening sky, the sizzling of the black Nilosian energy could be heard in the volley of the emerald green crackling power as it plowed into Orion.

His conjuration bellowed when the spell hit it. The gorilla's muscles bulged to twice the size they should have been. Crimson fur turned green. Red nails turned black and grew into jagged claws.

Orion roared with might as it powered up and recovered.

The purple gorilla struggled hopelessly.

Wanting to taste the victory first hand, Ben extended his thoughts for the reins. The magical control lit in the center of his mind and slapped against his palm, but he didn't grab on. Jack gaze was still vacant.

Ben bolted to Jack's body and dove on it.

He searched for, and found, his nylon spellcard holder. The six remaining cards sat snug in their elastic pockets.

Using both hands, Ben pried Jack's fist open and snagged his last spellcard.

He glanced to see how the fight was going.

Orion had the other gorilla down. His mouth cranked open when its shoulders arced back displaying a mouthful of serrated black teeth. Nearly a flash, it struck. Those horrid teeth dug into the purple's jugular.

Jack's gorilla winked from existence.

Jack, back in his body, kicked.

Ben's side lit with pain.

As Jack started to run, the thief's hand went to where he'd carried the spellcards, and came out empty.

Ben smiled. He took control of Orion and began to give chase.

Jack turned, his fingers twisting like the ogre at Meadows Towing had. He belted two hiss-gargled words, and forked bolts of purple energy shot from Jack.

The thief had cast without a spellcard or device. How? Ben dove Orion's body in front of his own

The magic pelted into Orion's side. The gorilla winced, groaned, and checked the wound.

Three baseball-sized holes had been burnt into Orion's side. A shudder flashed through the gorilla's body. An angry hoot rolled in his throat.

Besides the pressure of the impact and a slight tingle, none of the pain reached Ben. It was almost like being in a first-person shooter.

Jack started to cast.

Orion launched at the thief.

Jack jammed his wrists together.

Chains rattled behind Orion.

Ben seized control and turned.

The stable chain, now an incandescent purple, had broken free and snaked halfway to them. Its far end stuck in midair, the rest lashed out with great clamor.

Orion ducked under it.

Ben took control and grabbed the chain.

The extra length in the center arced out.

As he had wound rope on the docks, Ben looped a length around an elbow. In no time, he had it tight and straining against the unseen anchor. Using every augmented muscle fiber in the gorilla's body, Ben yanked.

The last link cracked open. Instead of reverting to magical energy and dispersing, the chain changed natures. It went from striking viper to crushing constrictor. The loops Ben thought he had, turned out to have him.

He spun once, swung the remaining length over his head like a lariat, and let it go in Jack's direction.

The chain hooked out toward the thief.

Jack almost leapt over it.

He would've been clear it if the chain hadn't arched up and wrapped his legs.

Jack crumpled to the ground with a wholly satisfying crunching thud.

To free Orion's arm, Ben pulled at the loops.

The chain wanted both of them.

A swell of magic—what the heck was that— expanded within Orion. Jarred, Ben tried to analyze it. Did Jack have a way of stealing control of conjurations?

Another surge of Nilosian energy filled every inch of his conjuration. The control reins vanished and Ben found his consciousness flung back into his own body. How was that possible? Orion was his spell. He'd cast it.

Uncontrolled. Orion ignored the chains to rush Jack. It dropped both fists on Jack's ribs. Muffled cracks punctuated the air as furry fists pounded further into a body than whole bones would allow.

Jack jabbered nonsensical cries. The chain vanished.

Ben gave a practice blink to dismiss the gorilla.

The green and red energies obeyed. They stripped themselves away and dissipated into swirling motes, but the black...

The serrated teeth and jagged claws kept their shape. A faint shadow—translucent Nilosian energy— held a vaguely gorilla-ish silhouette that loomed over Jack. Sprung wide like a steel trap, the black teeth chomped down on Jack's casting arm.

The thief's screams rose higher. He writhed and tried to pull free. The struggle made the teeth sink further which spurred Jack to higher screeches and further hysterics.

Mouth perfectly dry, the heady tang of fresh blood—how'd he know the taste?—gushed into Ben's mouth.

Reeling from the conjurer's link, Ben snapped it shut and focused on dismissing the teeth and the claws.

They resisted. No. They fought back, struggling hard—*punish the betrayer, make the false friend pay*—to remain. To finish.

Ben rubbed his forehead to expel the dark thoughts. They weren't his. That's not how he felt. It couldn't have been.

The teeth...the claws...turned to ash, then smoke.

Both bones in Jack's forearm broken, his wrist and hand dangled by white sinew. The bones showed white for an instant before blood washed over. Mangled arm cradled, Jack wailed and shrank away.

Trying to clear his mouth of the ghastly coppery taste, Ben forced himself to salivate and spat repeatedly.

Two stronghold guards, decked in red leather shot past. They leapt on Jack, rolled him face down, and secured him in thumbscrews.

Chapter Twenty-One

ON BEING A MESSENGER

JACK CAPTURED, the Redblades—Ben would have to find out their real title instead of referring to the Komir guards by The Friendship's slang—brought Ben in to stand next to Elder Komir's throne-chair at the end of a series of grid-set, long oaken tables. The redblade missing his left pinky called it the dining room. From the head of the room, Ben figured this *dining room* could hold the entire Archon Private Academy's cafeteria with room to spare.

Zesty foreign spices hung in the air. Besides the light rattling of the man's chainmail as he left, the room seemed to eat noise.

Alone, Ben wondered how much trouble he'd gotten himself into. He had his stuff back. However, in having gone after Jack, he went against what Elder Komir had *suggested*—her way of *telling*—him to do.

Trying to distil everything he knew about the elder, his imagination geared up to play *Guess the Reprimand*.

Before round one began, Elder Komir bustled into

the room. Her red, gold-trimmed robes whisked faint pink dust. "My young Baxter, I need to send you back to relay a message to your Master and only to him."

Ben frowned at having to tell Master Reynolds that he'd disobeyed someone of equivalent rank to his Master. "I'd rather take whatever punishment you have for me."

Elder Komir paused.

Dressed in similar robes, Penelope, who he hadn't seen enter behind the Elder, moved a step beyond her great-grandmother.

The Elder asked, "Punishment?"

Thrilled not to be in trouble, Ben smiled.

Penelope on her heels, Elder Komir hurried to close the distance. Her solemn expression remained fixed. She presented a golf ball sized metal orb. "The Node is under attack. We have discovered who is behind the offensive."

Ben's smiled waned. He gave a serious nod.

"It all started with the ogre kidnapping me." Penelope added, "The key is probably in the room where I was kept."

"No." Contradicting her, Elder Komir handed Ben the cool sphere. "Your Master will know what it looks like."

Her opinion dismissed, Penelope's brow furrowed.

"From what she explained of the monster—" Komir laid a soft, loving hand on Penelope's shoulder. "The Ogre Magi is probably wearing it like a charm." She removed the hand to palm the top half of the sphere. "He's fond of turning to gaseous form if the tide of the fight turns against him." Her wrinkled lips turned in disgust. "Once it goes gaseous, your Master will be able to capture the monster with this Encapsulating Orb."

"Okay." Ben nodded to both of them and found himself sinking into Penelope's blue eyes.

Breaking the eye contact, Elder Komir stepped between them. "Time is of the essence."

Ben nodded. His eyes flicked to Penelope when she moved around her great-grandmother. Did she like him, too?

Instead of regaining eye contact, Penelope's gaze went to the orb.

Ben took the small sphere with both hands. To be sure he recapped, "Tell Master Reynolds *The Node is under attack* and *the ogre at Meadows Towing is a part of it*. Give him this." He shook the orb. "To capture the monster when it turns into gas."

"Precisely." Elder Komir nodded. The lines on her serious brow twisted a bit. Concern? She said, "The door to Pepperjacks is not safe right now. To get you back, I'm going to have to Banish you."

Banish sounded like she said it with a capital B. Making it sound—capital B—Bad.

His eyes turned to Penelope. Ben's mental fortitude and resolve began to double. He nodded to Elder Komir. "Let's do it."

"I cannot put you at your school, but I can put you near your car."

A tentative fear fluttered into Ben's gut. Relenting to spells went again everything the Archon Private Academy taught. Yes, there were some good spells out there, but an instinctual resistance made his stomach tighten. Focusing through it, he nodded.

This, she projected to him, pushing her sleeves back to reveal liver-spotted arms. *Is going to hurt.*

Ben shot Penelope a confident, playful grin and dragged it to the Elder. "Hit me."

Faint golden energy played amongst the crimson as she began chanting in a hiss-gargling language. Her hands turned circles. Argosian energy trailed. Gold—unnamed, unknown energy—counter pointed from her index fingers. *Time is of the essence.*

Ben tried to ask about the new energy, but Elder Komir directed her spell at him.

A wave of yellow-traced red magic washed the Komirs, and the room, away.

Chapter Twenty-Two

BANISHED

THE BRILLIANT RED flash clamped Ben's eyes shut. Each muscle fiber in his being seared and went slack.

He fell on hard ground.

His noodley muscles came back to life with a tight constriction. Cramped and twitching, they seized in violent spasms.

Trying to find a way to flee, the Argosian energy in his veins—newly awoken by the Elder herself— expanded into needle-tip spikes. Wanting to seep from his ears, eyes, and nose, the vengeful energy in his head —the black stuff—had turned to fire, broiling his brain.

Ben tried to release them. To stop the pain, he'd let both go. Neither fled. Betraying him, his body held them in.

His legs kicked.

Teeth gnashed.

Back convulsed.

Ben's fingers tried to dig into the unyielding surface —concrete—beneath him.

The pain lessened enough for slight awareness to register. A coppery taste—blood—filled the right side of his mouth. He had chomped down on the inside of his cheek.

Elder Komir had mentioned the spell would *hurt*. Clearly their pain thresholds were vastly different. She should've said *writhing twinges* or *agonizing pain*.

The red light faded. The ground's coolness pressed through his coat. His legs occasionally twitched, and his arms had gone asleep.

Laying there, he opened his eyes.

Bright white filled his vision.

The light faded and tightened into florescent tubes locked behind protective grates. Beyond them, the concrete ceiling gently sloped away to hundreds of empty parking spots.

When he turned his head, he nearly came face to face with matte black metal. He lay next to the passenger side of his Transcend.

"Was that a new dance?" A synthesized voice —Tex—asked.

The back spasms ceased, but Ben's legs stayed as useless as his limp arms. Ben's gaze raked his companion, who wore one of the junkyard boar's spiked collar twisted to cover both shoulders like dual bandoleers. His companion stood on the dashboard and surveyed him with an expression of mild amusement.

"Once I heard you," Tex continued. "I started recording. You know, so you can watch it later... Maybe add music?"

Inhaling deeply, Ben noted something in the air. He stayed where he lay as the magic in his system eased its assault. Fuzzy ants-crawling-across-his-flesh feeling started coming back into his arms and legs. Sore and dry, his throat choked the question, "How long—"

"Twelve seconds." Tex gave an enthusiastic nod. "All the way from the mindless grunts through the incoherent babbling."

Ben redefined agony to *so much pain as to not be aware of time.*

He sniffed the warm air. It held a long-burning, high-heat smell that reminded him of when he had to work the kiln during Glass Works II all those years ago. Slicking his throat with saliva and blood, he asked, "Do you smell smoke?"

"When the wind blows this way." Tex tapped the flat space above its mouth-shaped speaker box to remind Ben it didn't have a nose and pointed beyond the windshield. "My air quality sensors detect higher than normal levels of carbon which has been steadily increasing for several hours."

Almost good to go, Ben arched to see. Laying on the ground, a low concrete wall blocked direct view of whatever his companion motioned at, but something lit the Las Vegas night sky.

Keeping his hand pointed, Tex glanced to Ben. "Something inside Pepperjacks is on fire."

Ben sprang to his feet. Complete recovery not yet arrived, his legs buckled and he leaned on his door. He looked beyond the front of the car. They were on a higher floor of the parking garage and had a mighty fine view of Pepperjacks.

Mundane fire trucks surrounded the property, but did not approach the building.

Ben couldn't see flames, but steady plumes of smoke rose from the building's top floor.

Remembering why Komir had blasted him with the —capital B—Banishment spell, Ben snapped his fingers. "Master Reynolds." He pulled his Anvilsmith from his hip and pressed *Call*. The screen with his programmed numbers came up, but the device flashed *no signal*.

Tex's optics twisted. "Where'd you get that?"

Feeling better, Ben stood and tested his balance. Yup. Good. He turned his focus to Tex. "What are you talking about?"

The small robot pointed down to the glove box. "Look inside."

Ben flicked it open to see another Anvilsmith.

"When you didn't respond to my ping, I bypassed your silent mode, sorry, and heard a conversation." Tex shrugged. "None of the voices were yours, and so I tracked down your tablet."

Ben pulled the device out.

"I snatched it and returned to the car." Tex shrugged. "Figured if I got all the gifts together, you'd eventually come to us."

Nodding, Ben compared both devices. They were the same, all the way down to his arcane mark on the back. He woke the screens. The device he had with him still showed ninety-nine arcane watts while the device Tex had in the glove box only had thirty-four. He eyed Tex. "Where did you find this again, exactly?"

His companion pointed to Pepperjacks. "Tucked into a booth eight in from the main entrance, against the wall. Two adults were, uh, *getting busy* in it."

Recalling when Collins had patted him down, Ben

bit his lip to stifle the string of expletives he wanted to use. Feeling them about to fly free anyway, he bit harder.

If he ranted about the blond bastard, Tex would report him for slandering a higher-ranking caster. At least that's what the first page of the manual said would happen. Part helper. Part guide. Part tracker. If only he could find a way to make the robot one-hundred percent ally.

Pushing Collins further from his mind, for now, Ben pressed call. As with the other device, the screen showed his contacts, but flashed no signal.

On both, he tapped *System*, *Diagnostics*, and *Run*.

"Tex, ping out to the APA." Ben dropped the tablets into the passenger seat and went around his car and got in. "I need to get a message to Master Reynol— Shit!" Patting his pockets, Ben searched around.

Tex asked, "What are you doing?"

"An orb! I had an orb." Ben focused on his companion. "A metal sphere about the size of a golf ball. Did you see one?"

Tex pointed. "It rolled to the wall and stopped over there."

Ben followed the tiny finger to see the Encapsulating Orb propped against a beer bottle. He went to get it. "Ping out."

"I can't." Tex looked from Ben to the devices in the passenger seat. His optical lenses twisted. "My pings are relayed through the tablet. If it cannot get a connection, I can't connect either."

Ben retrieved the sphere. It felt colder. He put it in his pocket, went back to his car, and dropped into the driver's seat. From Pepperjacks, Meadows Towing was a twenty minutes out toward Pahrump. If he didn't hit traffic, the Archon Private Academy—out by Sam Boyd Stadium—would be a forty-minute drive in almost the opposite direction.

Pepperjacks continued to smoke.

Time is of the essence, Elder Komir's words rang back.

He leaned over and clipped the tablet Tex had stashed in the glove box into the center council. He left the other in the seat. "When the tablets come up, Tex, do a deep check on both of them."

"Will do." Tex unclipped the spiked collar, hooked the ends into grooves on the dashboard, and hung in front of the console.

Ben took a moment to admire the rig. While it wasn't a perfect fit, it was ingenious. He'd have to see if something like that was on the market, it not, he would make the harness himself. "Tell me where they vary and try to get a signal."

Tex nodded.

Ben clicked his seatbelt on, started the car, and peeled out toward the exit.

Chapter Twenty-Three

24-SEVEN

HAVING STOPPED at the last 24-Seven convenience store on the edge of town, Ben tried using a mundane payphone to call the school.

As the phone rang and rang, cars zoomed along the Las Vegas Strip going into, or coming from, the city's main attraction. The line picked up. "Thank you for calling—"

Ben pumped his fist and spoke quickly. "Yes, this is Benjamin Bax—"

With even tones, the voice continued, "The Archon Private Academy. No one is here—"

Ben slammed the scarred receiver home on the graffitied cradle. He had expected to reach the on-duty Councilor, but got a message machine. "What's the point of having a twenty-four-hour hotline that goes to voicemail?"

Still on task, Tex's voice came from the passenger seat, "Did you leave a message?"

Ben grabbed his hair and walked to the Transcend. "Elder Komir said, specifically, to deliver the message only to Master Reynolds."

"Hmp, a conundrum." Tex turned its attention from the tablets and reported, "Several subroutines should not have been running on the tablet you had on your person, but both Anvilsmiths are identical from serial numbers to lack of connectivity. I stopped the subroutines and cleared them out, but cannot do anything about getting signal."

A 24-Seven store attendant, in his orange and red bowling shirt uniform, shoved someone with offensive body odor from the store. "Get out of here, you bum!" In a huff, the attendant rushed back inside.

The bum stumbled, recovered, and jutted a middle finger over his shoulder. He pulled a frosty tall can of beer from a pocket, cracked it, and started to drink.

Ben leaned on his Transcend, crossed his arms, and reassessed.

Only if he could've coded a real teleportation spell instead of the curriculum-mandated *Pop*. He'd be able to flash to the school and, if unable to find Master Reynolds, flash to Meadows Towing.

All teleports—all the really dope spells—were explored at the Advanced Spell Programming level. More than ever, he looked forward completing regular Spell Programming X.

Ben rubbed his face. Only if the Councilor would've answered...

It might've taken some serious conversational acrobatics to prove an emergency without stating the exact situation, but Master Reynolds would've teleported to him for full disclosure. Ben would have had a chance to explain everything and, hopefully, be done with the whole entire mess.

But the Councilor didn't answer.

Having gone toward Meadows Towing, it'd be an even longer drive to the school now. Sunday. Ben heaved an angry sigh. The school, besides the on-duty Councilor—who wasn't worth a doodie right now—always stood vacant on Sundays.

The Node is under attack. We have discovered who is behind the offensive...wearing the key like a charm...time is of the essence.

Ben realized his leg had started to shake. He had to do something. Every bit of him knew it.

In watching the bum walk further away, still drinking his tall beer, Ben began to nod to himself. He didn't have to take down Meadows Towing or the Krotosian. He only had to get the key.

He spun and pointed to the tablet in the passenger seat. "Start channeling all the arcane wattage from that device—" He pointed to the one latched on the console. "Into this one."

"Transferring arcane wattage from—"

"I know," Ben interrupted. He slid into his car. Tex had started giving him the same spiel Rembrandt had given him a few years ago when Erik—his lab partner during Spell Programming IV—needed some extra energy to pass Applicable Magic II. He started the car. "I'd just use that one, but it's cursed."

Tex tilted its head, a move Ben believed it learned

from him. "Still, transferring arcane wattage from device to device is not optimal usage. There will be a twenty-five percent loss, and the process will take nearly ten minutes."

Ben nodded to the timetable in his head. He'd be at Meadows Towing in fifteen. "Yes, that's fine. Please do it."

The little robot's hands folded back to reveal a microSD extension on each wrist. Tex stopped. "You do not have authority to approve such a waste."

Thankful the robot couldn't read thoughts, Ben pressed his lips together and paraphrased the second page of the manual—it was as far as he'd gotten before the day span out of control. "As a Junior Apprentice, I'm allowed one override, with which you have to comply. The override will be reviewed and either approved or disapproved by my Councilor." Ben focused on his companion. "Texas, buddy, I *really* don't want to override you."

The robot's head dropped for a half-second before it slid one of its wrist-jacks into an Anvilsmith.

Figuring the half-second pause must've been the equivalence of Tex's processors giving the thought thirty minutes of consideration, Ben smiled at the outcome.

Tex's shoulder disconnected. A cord extended from the socket as it leaned over to plug the other wrist into the second Anvilsmith in the car seat. "I would rather not be overridden."

Ben smiled. "Texas, you're the best companion anyone could hope for."

Tex nodded, shone green and began to slowly

pulsate light. Arcane watts transferred from one tablet, to Tex, and then into the device.

Too late to change his mind or stop Tex, Ben wondered if the curse Collins installed on the tablet would transfer along with the energy.

Chapter Twenty-Four

SCRAPYARD REPRISE

BEN KILLED the headlights before he turned onto the unnamed dirt road which led to Meadows Towing. From here he could see the shadowy blot of its silhouette standing out against the distant hills on the dark desert floor. He killed the engine and coasted to a stop half a mile away from the scrapyard.

Sucking in a deep inhalation of clean desert air, Ben held it, tried not to think about what he planned on doing, and let it out. He spat his grape gum into its spent wrapper and tucked it into the ashtray.

Crickets started to chirp.

A click next to him—the glove box—gave the insects a moment pause as Tex pulled out something that scraped as it left the glove box.

Ben leaned in to see the thin thing by the faint green glow of Tex's eyes. A second spiked collar? "What am I to do with that?"

Tex lifted it toward him. "Wear it."

Ben took the leather strap and carefully turned the spiked collar over in his hands. "Why?"

Tex tapped its own spiked collar, wrapped around shoulders and waist. "If these blocked Chrystal from being able to see the boars in her divination, it stands to reason that it should keep anyone from seeing you." His companion pointed at the tablet on the left. "That one is full, the other should be put away."

Ben nodded and held the collar around his neck.

It snapped close and cinched.

He tugged at it.

It loosened at his pull and tightened again when he released it. The boars had massive necks. The collar should hang loose.

Ben pulled at it one last time.

It came back tight.

He sighed and relented. He'd heard that the Red Rock Witch had worn a foreign necklace—the fabled Nether-Choker—only once and when sunlight hit her, she transformed from whatever she was before the necklace turned her into the distant rotting hag she was rumored to be.

To be safe, he'd have this thing off well before sunrise.

Tex climbed to the top of the car door and leapt. Ben locked up, got out, and scooped up his Anvilsmith. He tapped *Maps* and noticed the path they were taking now was nearly the same as when they originally came to Meadows Towing. Hoping his bicycle would still be where he left it, he thoughtlessly gave the collar another pull. "Lead on."

It cinched tight.

Ben eyes started to adjust to the night as his companion led him across the dark desert floor before coming to a stop.

Tex said, "We're a hundred yards out." The green dot that represented where Ben had left his bike disappeared. "And consider your bike stolen."

Ben refused to mope. He had a car now.

The tall, rotating, star-shaped Meadows Towing sign, which had shed lavender-white light like a lighthouse the night before, stood as a silent sentry. All the lights were out. The moon barely lit the hardpan, and Ben recognized the maze more by the shadows cast by the towering wrecked cars.

Ben tried to recall the path he took a couple of nights ago...Too many turns. Too many dead ends. He shook his head. So much for the easy way.

Tex asked, "Did you mark the car?"

"Yes." To prove it to himself, he stole a glance at his tablet and nodded at the small red dot there.

"So," Tex looked from him into the scrapyard. "Are we going the way I went to the center building or the long meandering way you took?"

Meandering? Ben pointed. Exasperation filled his voice. "You ran across the top of the rows."

"Not my fault you'd make too much noise."

Ben pinched the screen. The overview he created before their first adventure into Meadows Towing came up. Two paths ran from where they were to the center. Tex must've tracked their movement.

About to bathe Tex with compliments, Ben bit his lip. A blue line, with *winner Tex* repeated along the length, took a near direct path to where the Transcend had been stored in the work bays. Ben's route, yellow— stamped *non-winner Ben*—showed the way he'd taken to the building.

Companions' personalities were supposed to become a caricature of the owner traits, but Ben never thought of himself as competitive. He'd be more mindful to notice that trait in the future so he could keep it in check.

He tapped the screen. A lime-green line lit under his fingertip and he traced his past path. He short-cutted the dead ends and skipped the loop he made to avoid a boar.

Before he could present the path to Tex, his companion nodded. "Got it."

Though his tablet and the robot were distinctly separate devices, Ben marveled at how well they synced.

Ben tapped *Spells*, the *Enchantments* icon, and then *Elf Sight*.

He had begrudged having to build it in Spell Programming VI and lamented the lost time he could've spent programming productive spells. Aside from proving that it worked during his final, Ben never imagined he would actually be casting the spell. Inwardly he had bet against it.

Ben resented the spell so much that he hadn't designed a background and used the default *Cast* button. A lone slider—*Duration*—lay under the glass. Ben slid it to the far right. An hour. Enough time to get in, try to sneak the key, and get out. The *Cast* button flashed a -5 below it. He'd have ninety-five arcane watts left.

Looking from his device to the sky, Ben slid his mouthpiece in and took a moment to note the constellations.

Even this far from the city, Las Vegas washed out many of the weaker stars, leaving the stronger celestial bodies alone in the night sky. A small part of him wanted to return to the Komir spire just to look up at the universe.

Ben shook the fantasy from his head. If he didn't act now, Pepperjacks would burn down and ruin any chance he had of ever getting back to the other side to see the stars—or Penelope—again.

He tapped the plain *Cast* icon.

The Anvilsmith vibrated weakly in his hands for a brief second. Then nothing.

"Don't give me that." He knew a dud when he felt one and shook the device. "I ran the program through a debugger..." For a moment, he wondered if he had accidentally loaded an earlier version of the spell. No. He'd remember that. Ben shook the tablet again. "There's nothing wrong with the coding—"

A hundred feet away, a beam of white light shot down from the sky.

Fearing an attack, Ben froze, and searched.

Tex moved to his side. "What?"

In the distance, another single beam of light came from the sky.

Ben pointed. "There."

Tex asked, "Where?"

Dual beams of light dropped down. Then seven. Then more and more.

Ben turned his face to the sky.

The washed out stars lit brilliantly in the night. It seemed like each distant heavenly body twinkled. The brighter ones leaked light which fell on the desert floor like ephemeral rain.

He held out his hand.

The light didn't have a feel to it, but bounced and splashed on his palm like water. *So fricking cool!* Ben cupped his hand, but the splatters of light evaporated before it could pool.

He'd only ever cast the spell in the clinically-lit classroom. His device had shocked magic into him, and Collins had sneered at having to give Ben an A.

Now, through the sheets of light, Meadows Towing —the ground, the wrecked cars, the sign above the scrapyard, even the prison-like bars spanning the thirty feet between concrete columns—glimmered as though they were wet.

Planning to enter the way he had before, Ben swiped back to his other enchantments and tapped the kangaroo icon. He had extra time in Courtmanship IV, so he rewrapped his jumping spell. "Hmm. Missed changing the main icon." He'd gone back and forth between a tarsier and a flea—since fleas could also jump ridiculously far for their size—but the small simian, with its bugged eyes, won out.

Ben puzzled at the grayed-out duration bar. The slider defaulted to the top, wanting to give him the full ten minutes for one arcane watt. "It should cost three."

"What?" Tex asked.

"Tarsier." Ben swiped from the spell. Investigating, he called up his speed spell. The background of the spell had *Usain Bolt* running through a finish line, arms raised in a vee, over it, a grayed-out duration bar with a highly italicized *Cast* with speed streaks trailing left. For ten minutes, a *-1* lit behind *Cast* instead of the normal *-3*. Maximum duration for an *awatt*. "And Usain is only one too."

He turned the Anvilsmith over. The magical sigil—his name arched in lightning around his studious version of the APA's gorilla mascot—flashed at him. He lowered the tablet to show it to Tex. "This is the one from Pepperjacks, right?"

Tex looked the tablet over for a moment. Probably way longer than it needed to. "Yes." It angled its pale green orbs up at Ben. "Why?"

"*Usain* and *Tarsier* say they only need one *awatt* to cast top-slide. Each is supposed to be three." Ben rubbed his chin and frowned at the device. "The spells are acting funny."

Was it possible that Tex had stolen Senior Adept Collins' tablet when he snuck in, instead of recovering the correct tablet? If Tex had, why would Collins have any arcane mark besides his own on his tablet?

Thinking of the duplicate inscription on the second Anvilsmith, Ben shook his head. The jerk already slipped him one, maybe he was planning to switch it out again.

Feeling a bit paranoid, Ben made a mental note to come up with a different way of marking his device since—despite what teachers and counselor said—the *Inscription* spell could obviously be faked.

Another task for another time.

Ben swiped out and tapped *Tarsier*. He activated the

thick block cast button made to look like small simian's bugged eyes.

As before, the Anvilsmith merely vibrated in his hands, indicating the spell had failed. A moment later, a powerful infusion of magic washed over him and pulsed into his legs—sinking into his muscles.

The spell had cast, it didn't hurt, and only cost one *awatt*. Something was going on, but what?

Chapter Twenty-Five

DEADLY GROUND

"GRAB ON, TEX." Ben strode forward across the starlight-bathed desert hardpan to the thirty-foot column he had jumped up to before. Meadow's Towing steel-laden air filled his nose. In the distance, a coyote howled.

He eyed the protruding stone lip. Tex's weight registered on his coat. Ben squatted, aimed, and leapt.

Before, with all of his effort, his fingers barely hooked over the top. This time, he scraped his knee on the edge as he overshot the lip by ten feet and landed on the flat top.

Tex asked, "How'd you do that, Ben?"

He shrugged. "Has anything like this ever been reported before?"

"I still don't have connectivity, so I can't check, but we're programmed with thousands of situations that are likely to happen to young casters—" Tex looked to where Ben had leapt from. "And there's nothing like this in my memory stores."

Be asked, "Do you have to report that this happened?"

"No." Tex shook its head. "You have me in companion mode so I'm able to keep secrets. You'd just have to tag the occurrence as private."

"Good." Ben narrowed his eyes to carefully choose his wording. "For the record, Tex. Consider anything I do with magic, private."

"Nice!" Tex nodded. "Excellent blanket coverage."

Atop the thirty-foot concrete column, Ben scanned the starlight-bathed scrapyard. Thanks to his *Elf Sight* spell, the darkness of night had retreated to a soft, sunny day. When he gazed out into the desert, the brightness gave way at a certain point to a distant curtain of night. "So cool."

Noting his path through the general pattern of the main aisles among the dozens of rows of wrecked cars, Ben leapt down. He set Tex on the ground, and jogged to the first main aisle. Nearing the end of the row, Tex advised, "You should get a spell ready."

Not looking down, Ben flashed Tex a glimpse of the Orion SD card he had in his hand. "Got one."

"But your Anvilsmith is hanging on your hip." His companion pointed. "It should be in your hand."

"I'm good, Tex. Thanks." He spared his companion a wink and a confident smile. "Help me keep an eye out for the boars."

They hustled across to the rows on the other side.

Tex picked up his pace to get a lead. At the edge of the next row, it peeked around the corner. Its little robot arm went up.

Ben stopped. His grip tightened on the SD card. He eyed Tex's arm and listened.

A soft steady wind whistled through the wrecks and pushed the collected smell of neglected plastic and steel into his face. At last, a faint gruff voice barked foreign words.

Keeping Tex in his peripheral vision, Ben pulled his Anvilsmith. He tapped *Options*, *Translate*, and *To Text*. The screen went blank. It couldn't register the distant words. Splitting his attention between the Anvilsmith and Tex's arm, Ben crept down the row toward the corner.

The black screen now showed a small green sound wave dancing below the registration point. The voice had grown a little louder, but the mic on his device wasn't sensitive enough.

The robot's arm stayed raised.

Just shy of the corner, the device flashed *Orc to English*. Ben focused on the sentence as it appeared. "Say what you want, but this is bullshit."

The voice sounded close. Almost too close.

Ben looked from the screen. Tex had disappeared. No, the robot had crouched under the crushed front fender at the corner car. The little robotic arm shook like an air pressure needle, directing him back, back, back.

Ben back-pedaled.

Halfway down the row, Tex's hand turned sideways.

Ben stopped and tried to flatten his body against the wall of wreckage towering over him. Points of metal kept him from leaning too far back.

The sloped facial profile of an orc—with a Bluetooth

device flashing in its ear—came into view and turned away to walk the perimeter.

Its broad shoulders were rounded forward and its head hung low. Barefoot, it wore a large sword strapped across its white t-shirt clad back, and a holstered gun bounced on its right jean-covered hip. It barked Orcish, but the orc's steps were sulking tromps seemed overly pouty.

Tex waved him forward and gave hand signs to come fully around the corner.

Doing as suggested, Ben stayed close to the wreckage, but not so close as to snag his coat on something, and slunk around the corner.

Tex moved out to scout the length of the next row.

About to read the orc's translated text, two groups of words both had a pop-up. *Might-Fist* and *Shame-Feast*.

Might-Fist (n.) A title used amongst goblinoids and wild races to denote the ruler of a vast region. One Might-Fist may have many lesser Fists who help control the area.

Ben didn't tap *Fists*. Context told him what it meant.

Shame-feast (v.) A ritual called by overlords after pitting failed minions against each other in an honor battle. When a Shame-feast is called, the victor of the honor battle must immediately do the following or be slain.

Ben recalled honor battle from before. He read the first of five bullet points.

The victor is to eat the feet of the fallen foe.

Ben envisioned the horrific act and grimaced. His stomach constricted. Without hesitation, he tapped the tiny *x* at the corner. *Shame-feast* highlighted as a hyperlink and the pop-up vanished.

The mental image of the grisly bullet point tried to force its way into his imagination. Ben shook his whole body to slip the vision in disgust.

Tex motioned him forward.

Ben moved up behind his tiny companion who—of course—had been right about the need to keep his Anvilsmith at the ready. While he'd be ready to cast if he needed a creature, he'd be a half-second behind being prepared if he needed another spell.

In Introduction to Dueling, Adept Love always went on and on about how a half-second could be the difference between life and death. Though Ben had dismissed the tired warning in class, he now understood why the Adept drilled it.

Best to prepare.

Pop, his short range teleportation spell, would be the quickest way to keep from being spotted. Ben swiped the transcription away, tapped *Spells*, and then the fat exclamation point icon to get to *Conjurations*.

He came to the corner just in time to come face-to-chest with a different orc turning onto his row.

Ben gazed up into its black irises and found no space for love there.

The orc took a quick half step back. Dressed like the other, its massive green hands went to the gun on its hip. It frowned. Then went for the sword.

Ben rolled backwards over his left shoulder to get some distance and channeled Argosian energy into the spell card.

His hand flashed red before he finished the roll.

A tiny clap of thunder sounded Orion's appearance,

scarlet fur over ruby skin. The red gorilla caught the orc's arms on the downstroke.

Ben had never materialized a creature so fast.

The blade stopped just above his head.

Taller than his earlier casting, the crimson Orion stood eye-to-eye with the orc.

The orc dropped a hand from the hilt toward his hip.

Squatting, Ben took control of Orion. He caught hold of the orc's wrist just shy of the gun.

The orc grunted. It tried to force the sword hand down into Ben's comatose body while also trying to force its other hand toward the gun.

Recalling a lesson from Adept Love's *Surviving Brutes* combat class, Ben stopped pushing against the orc. Instead, he turned Orion's hips into the creature, pulled both arms down and tucked his toward his torso.

The orc flipped over. Slapped flat on its back, the orc's breath came out in a hard puff.

Ben tried to think what to do next and realized he'd accidently stalled Orion. He let Orion act on its own.

Raining blows, they dropped on the orc.

Tex called, "Your body!"

Ben turned Orion's head to glance.

The first, Bluetoothed orc had its sword out and angled back as it charged down the row at Ben's limp body.

Chapter Twenty-Six

DOUBLE THE TROUBLE

BEN EJECTED FROM ORION. The gorilla's adrenaline— through piggybacking on its senses—always felt dull and distant. In his own body, Ben's heart thumped and his muscles keyed for action.

His eyes tried to make sense of his surroundings. That's right, he had squatted.

Feet thumped behind him. Drawing closer.

He glanced beyond the orc coming behind him with its sword cocked back over its head. Popping to the other side of the junked cars would provide complete safety, but he'd lose precious line of sight of Orion and the gorilla would disappear.

He tapped *Pop*.

The Anvilsmith gave a worryingly weak vibration.

The sword came down.

Ben reappeared behind the Bluetoothed orc, who stabbed at the air around where Ben had been. The orc must've thought he had gone invisible.

No sooner had he thought about sending Argosian

energy through the Orion spellcard still in his hand, did his hand flash red and—with a faint thunderclap—a second red gorilla appeared.

The Bluetoothed orc had just started to shift its weight from a missed attack at an invisible foe to look back when the second Orion slammed it into the wall of jagged points from compacted cars.

His gorilla gripped Bluetooth around the waist, lifted the orc—pulling it away from the compacted metal it tried to grasp onto—arced its simian back to heave the orc over its body and slam Bluetooth into the hard packed earth.

"A suplex?" Ben gaped at the wrestling move.

The gorilla then rolled over the limp orc, picked it up in a belly-to-belly bear hug and arched back to suplex-spike Bluetooth's head into the ground again.

A horrifying crunching crack made Ben shudder.

The back of the orc's head had, for a split-second, made full contact with its back.

Mouth agape, Ben found his head had tilted in wonder. He corrected his neck and shut his mouth.

The first Orion grabbed its orc's sword with its foot, tossed the sword toward its shoulder, transferred control of the orc's wrist from hand to foot, caught the hilt of the weapon in the air, and drove it down into the orc's chest.

Ben found his jaw unhinged again and let it be. Where had they learned that stuff?

The two gorillas rolled their dead orcs over and were grunting to each other. The Second Orion pulled the Bluetooth device from the broken necked orc's ear, sniffed it, and let out a small grunt before tossing it to the side.

As though responding, the First Orion echoed the grunt. It pulled a knife from the orc that Ben had not seen, then gave a hoot and a grunt.

The Second Orion went to the orc's hip to pull a knife from its scabbard. It grunted twice, and tossed that scabbard dagger to the first. Then, it pulled the sword free from the limp body and gave two quick hoots.

The First Orion stood up, knife in hand and swung it back and forth as it recovered the knife tossed its way.

His conjurations' actions gave Ben goose bumps. He inched toward them, recognizing what they were doing. "No. Flipping. Way."

Between the grunts and different weapon choices, Ben realized these gorillas were not two versions of Orion working in unison, but two entirely different beings, communicating about what could be worthwhile.

They were looting the bodies.

Ben closed his mouth. "Amazing." He motioned toward the two as they swapped bodies and continued their search. He asked Tex. "Has anything like this ever been documented before now?"

"No." Tex shook its head. It moved to Ben, arcing wide and away from the gorillas. "I don't have record of anyone being able to cast red creatures."

"What? No, I meant the looting?" Ben considered Tex's response. Besides his red gorillas and Jack's purple one, all summoned creatures were supposed to be green. What had changed? For a moment, Ben wondered how the tablets were able to tap into the emerald power.

Elder Komir had gifted him a reserve of the red magic. The Argosian font of power in his chest. That's what changed. A jubilant rumble filled his heart and lungs. He wanted to roar in happiness that he actually belonged to a color of magic.

The quiet and cold smell of steel pressing in around him tamped his enthusiasm. This was not the time to yell in celebration. Later. He'd celebrate later.

The gorilla with the knives sniffed at the gun on the dead orc's hip.

Its fingers looked too thick to fit all the way into the trigger guard, but the tip could pull the trigger. If it did, shots would sound and ruin Ben's plan for stealth.

Ben froze and prepared to dismiss both of the gorillas.

Seemingly aware of his thoughts, the gorilla looked at Ben. Something—Ben couldn't quite put his finger on what—exchanged between them. The Orion then batted the gun away with an uninterested grunt.

The second gave a similar grunt before doing the same.

Appreciation spread a smile across Ben's lips. "They just read my intentions."

Tex asked, "How do you know?"

"I felt the first one acknowledge my concern about the guns." Feeling as though someone watched him, Ben checked behind him. Nothing. His smiled broadened further when he figured out how. "He used the Conjurer's Link as a guide."

"Oh." Tex had a way of turning away that showed

its total disinterest in the conversation. The robot did it now. It extended its eye sockets. "Since we're looting, their rings are magical."

Each gorilla lifted a hand and a sliver glint played on the thumb.

Ben asked, "You can detect magic?"

Tex's eye sockets twisted as they retracted. "Did you even touch the owner's manual?"

Each gorilla tossed a ring at Ben. He picked up the first one with a nod to the gorilla with the sword. "Thank you, Slash." Ben picked up the second ring and nodded to the knife-wielding gorilla. "Thank you, Slice."

They hooted softly at him.

Tex turned back to give Ben an apprising stare.

Ben defended his naming convention with a slight shrug. "What? They're obviously not Orion."

Tex gave a passing gesture toward them. "So you named them Slash and Slice?"

"They feel like verbs." Ben gave another a shrug. "How about Abe and Oscar?"

Tex went to the edge of the row to keep a look out. "Your conjurations. Your call."

Not sure how longsword-wielding Abe and knife-wielding Oscar would last, Ben started the group toward the main building.

Chapter Twenty-Seven

HOOTING AND LOOTING

THOUGH THEY HADN'T RUN into any further opposition, they maintained their system. Tex scouted, next—knives at the ready—Oscar walked in front of Ben, and Abe brought up the rear.

Hunkered down behind the final row of cars before the long gap of desert hardpan to Meadows Towing auto shop garages, Ben noted the silence and succulent smell of bacon before peeking at the building through gaps in the crushed cars.

The doors to the five car bays were closed. Darkness lay beyond the two large kitchen windows. *Elf Sight* functioned well under the stars, but would be useless inside the pitch-black building where the raining starlight couldn't splash.

Ben whispered, "The place seems too quiet."

Peering at the building, Tex matched the hushed down and agreed. "Yup, and no boars, either."

Guessing at the source of the delicious smell, Ben replied. "We probably won't see any."

Tex asked, "What makes you say that?"

Ben took in the scent again. "You don't smell the bacon?"

"I don't have a nose, Ben. Remember?" Tex gave an annoyed tap at the space between his eye sockets and mouth-shaped speaker box. As Ben started to feel silly for asking, the corners of Tex's lips kicked up to a smile. "Still, this smells like a trap."

Keeping his eyes on the building, Ben's finger tapped on the screen from memory to cue *Soul Sight*. He glanced at the slider, moved the range to six hundred feet, and narrowed his eyes.

Two things were wrong with his Anvilsmith. First, it showed him having eighty-nine arcane watts. *Pop* usually cost twenty, now—like the others—it cost much less. Even the cued *Soul Sight* typically cost five, but the indicator under the aura-like *Cast* icon showed -1.

He still couldn't figure out why everything suddenly became cheaper and more powerful. Pressing *Cast*, Ben gave a dismissive grunt. He'd figure it out later.

The device gave the lame-duck vibration then magic gently pulsed into his eyes.

Contemplating making his entrance through the door leading into the customer service area, Ben focused his spell to get a hint of what waited for him inside.

The last row of wrecked cars faded from view, leaving a vague outline marking where they were. Like he had x-ray vision, Ben could see the building through the cars. Then, as he focused on each wall in the building, they faded to outlines as his spell penetrated further, and further.

Large and purple, the only soul in range—the Krotosian—paced the room on the second floor. Ben couldn't help but wonder if it had picked up the turkey leg or left it to rot.

Elder Komir had said Master Reynolds would know what to do, what the key looked like. She also said that the Krotosian would probably be wearing it. In thinking about what he, not Master Reynolds, had to do, Ben found he'd moved so his elbows were at his side and his forearms formed a tight protective x across his chest.

The memory of Penelope trying to cover the multitude of various bruises and wounds on her arms and face with her blood-matted hair came into his mind's eye. He recalled the multiple rings of rope burns around her wrists. She didn't say, but he knew they had bound her hands together, hung her from the hook in the TV room, and beat her. They had been willfully able to viciously harm her. Heck, they probably considered it entertainment.

If he were to fail, Ben figured that he'd somehow be subjected to even worse brutalities and no one would be coming for him.

Oscar pulled on Ben's shoulder. The knife-wielding gorilla gave him three soft hoots. Giving two similar hoots, Abe bumped him from behind.

Almost forgetting they were there—surprised they hadn't winked out—Ben nodded to them. He had to do this or The Node would be destroyed or—as they said in the Beakless Griffin—controlled by a darker magic.

Ben set his jaw and scanned the building one more time.

The Krotosian still paced alone, but when he turned... When he turned, a small red light—the Node Key, it had to be the Node Key—lay on his wrist.

"Once we get through the service door, Tex, I want you to go to the far stairs and see what is up there." Ben nodded to Oscar and Abe with a determined grin. "We'll take care of the ogre magi."

Tex and the gorillas nodded back.

Ben glanced up at the distant stars raining light. He drew a deep breath of the bacon-slathered air. Striving to ignore it, Ben focused past the smells of cooking and neglected metal to get at the underlying desert air, and made a mental note to—after tonight—stop and appreciate the simple things in life.

"On three." His nerves bundled up in his guts. Fear threatened to arrest his body. A small part of him wanted to slink away. This Node business—this crazy, *crazy* ogre-fighting Node business—should be handled by his Master. Not him.

Gathering his courage, Ben counted, "One... two...

Chapter Twenty-Eight

INTO THE FRAY

"THREE."

Oscar went around the corner.

Heart pounding, Ben pushed through his mounting terror. He rounded the edge of wrecked cars. The smell of bacon smacked him. The silence felt deeper. The building appeared taller. Darker. His legs full of lead as his feet slapped hard to cross the long open space to Meadows Towing.

A quarter of the way across the clearing, his body got on board with his mind and loosened up.

A third of the way across the clearing, the Krotosian stopped pacing and turned their direction.

Halfway across the clearing, the five bay doors shot up with a rattling bang as though their counterbalances had broken. Starlight splashed just inside the darkened entrances, showing an orc at the mouth of each bay. Braced against their hips, a submachine gun.

Ben's bowels liquefied. His cheeks clenched to keep his poop in. He froze.

Oscar stopped, shifted his body and shielded Ben.

Muzzles flashed as gunfire cracked in small, controlled bursts.

A tapping lit on Ben's leg like he'd been hit by low-speed paintballs. Before his eyes, another tap pressed his slacks against his leg as a small, flattened, piece of metal fell from where he had been hit.

The locket around his neck warmed against his skin. More bullets—I should be Swiss cheese—squished flat against an invisible barrier before falling around his feet.

A mist—blood—came from Oscar's shoulders and sprinkled his face. Ben wiped and gawked at the crimson on his fingers.

Conjurations don't—weren't supposed to—bleed.

Ben's lips tightened. His nostrils flared. His brow knitted as he glared at the orcs. Argosian energy poured from him into the spell card. Gorilla after gorilla appeared next to the orcs in the bay.

Oscar had dropped to a knee after Ben had cast his second one.

The locket around his neck began to rise in temperature. A part of him equated it to how many more bullets pelted him.

Ben cast two more gorillas before feeling the dark energy in his brain start to press for release. The sinister energy abated when Oscar fell, but came right back banging at Ben's mental doors when he cast a fifth gorilla to engage the last orc.

The locket burned against his skin.

Ben yanked his tie loose, ripped the top of his shirt open, and stared at the Komir's talisman.

A purple flash lit around him, washing the world in an arcane glow.

The locket—fixed fire—lay one button lower, pressed against his skin. Trying to get at it, Ben stumbled.

A flash of purple lit behind him.

Ben spun.

Dirt filled the air as though something had shot at him from the roof of the building.

Remembering the Krotosian, Ben spun again.

A secondary effect from having both Soul Sight and Elf Sight going at the same time lit the ogre magi's form at the edge of the roof, making the creature a bright purple beacon against the raining starlight. Its body looked like an eldritch, stained-glass figure moving behind a thin waterfall.

As though in slow motion, Ben could see the magic happen.

Krotosian energy wavered in the center of the ogre's body, undulating from its core. The knotted violet mass rolled as a part of it slid up to the ogre's left shoulder, pulsed there for a moment, then dropped down to its hand to pulse again. A third pulse lit the ogre's hand before the purple energy fluttered to full intensity. Finally—flashing bright enough to be seen by Ben's natural vision—the Krotosian caster's hand hooked forward as it hurled another magic blast at him.

Seeing it coming, Ben kept his eyes on the ogre and ran his fingers along his cardholder. He stopped on the fourth SD card. Instead of pulling his *Shield* spell to slap it into his Anvilsmith, Ben channeled Argosian energy into it.

Where his tablet would normally make a physical green shield appear on his arm, the standard minty smell filled his nose, but no shield appeared. Mercifully, the burning locket on his chest cooled. Though there hadn't been a physical manifestation of the *Shield* spell, two years of combat practice made Ben's arm go up to block the incoming blast.

The purple energy dissipated against his forearm.

No impact. Weird. The locket on his chest started to heat up—the talisman pulled energy from his Argosian font—before cooling again. Aware, Ben felt the gorillas pull power from him, too, using him as a source to stay active.

The strain of power flowing through him from his dwindling Argosian reserve made a vein on his forehead.

Not having to move his arm to block incoming blasts, Ben tapped *Spells*, *Evocation*, then *Missile*. He aimed, and pressed *Cast*.

The Anvilsmith vibrated, lit green, before giving a slight kick as the bolt of emerald energy flew from his tablet.

It struck the purple stained-glass ogre, and pushed it away from the edge.

The Krotosian came back, then toppled over the ledge.

Victorious, Ben pumped his fist. "Yes!" A part of him —*too easy*—marveled at the violet body wreathed—*way too easy*—in green energy. The angle of the fall seemed off. A trick of the light, or magic—

Ben's eyes widened.

Flying, the Krotosian barreled at him.

Ben dove.

The ogre blew past in a powerful rush of air.

Like the *Shield* spell, the locket gave him protection in a casting duel, but, also like *Shield* spell, would probably be useless against physical assault.

Ben wanted to cast another gorilla, but five proved to be his limit and they were still engaged with the orcs.

The dark energy in his mind brimmed, offering full access to its untapped stores.

Recalling the teeth and shadowy form looming over Jack—and even more so his inability completely control the magic—Ben shook his head against the Nilosian energy.

The ogre looped and barreled through the air at him again.

Faking left, Ben dove right.

The ogre blew past again. Closer this time making his coat flap.

Ben tapped *Cast* three times.

The spell was cued. The tablet vibrated.

Ready for the kick, Ben grinned at the Krotosian.

The ogre spun in mid-air, turned to face Ben, and swiped his hand through the air three times. The lump of purple energy traveled from its gut to its shoulder, then to its hand.

Each motion caused the Anvilsmith to emit an annoying buzz as the spell's energy fizzled.

Ben's breath caught in his throat.

Eyes aglow with violet energy, the ogre landed, sneering its black teeth at Ben.

Fear grabbed a hard hold of Ben's guts and gave them a cruel shake. Again, he thought of the sinister teeth that had bit Jack. Then, he recalled how Jack had screamed as though his soul had been rendered.

Ben took a step back.

The ogre's derisive grin widened.

The fear that had taken hold of Ben's stomach branched out into his limbs telling him to *run*. To *get to safety*.

He'd heard of nullifying another caster's spell by channeling energy into the same spell, and focusing on canceling the magic, but no one ever wasted power on counter-spelling. In tournaments, you were always better served casting your own spell than to sap the opponent's energy.

Ready to counter-spell again, the ogre's lips peeled back further and it chomped at the air. It gave another predator's grin as it stalked toward Ben, salivating as it carefully started to close the distance to its prey.

Hoping to be faster, Ben tapped *Cast* again.

Purple energy moved up through the ogre's body and sucked the green from his tablet.

Taking another step back, Ben gained a new understanding of counter-spelling. In tournaments, if both casters ran out of energy, the match would be declared a draw.

This wasn't a tourney.

Ben didn't have to reach far to guess the hulking monster's tactic was to run him out of energy, then beat him to a bloody pulp—like it had Penelope—with its massive fists.

A vision of himself, hands bound, hanging from the hook like a punching bag rolled through his head.

Ben shook the image away. He wasn't going to let that happen, but how to stop it?

The Nilosian energy swam frantic circles in his head. At the ready. Looping.

Ben tightened his grip on the Orion spellcard. The Nilosian energy knew the path from his brain, down his arm, and into the card, but waited. He just had to release it.

The Krotosian lifted from the ground. It must've sensed the coming change of spells. Charging, it growled.

Ben turned the energy loose.

It flashed down his arm and sizzled into the spell card. There, the Nilosian energy didn't flash black in his hand. No, more to the point, it absorbed raining starlight in the area around him and plunged Ben into darkness.

Chapter Twenty-Nine

WAKING THE BEAST

UNLIKE THE ARTIFICIAL, uninvolved feeling of casting through a tablet or having to tap into the Argosian energy in his chest, Ben found focusing Nilosian energy from his mind into the card felt graceful. No. *Natural*.

Roaring into being, Bastion, a pitch black, nine-foot-tall four-armed gorilla, materialized next to him. A sour smell—spoiled milk—filled Ben's nose

The raining starlight returned, lighting the desert earth around him. For an exhilarated moment, Ben thought they had teleported outside Meadows Towing to safety. Then the first row of stacked, decimated cars came into view.

His thoughts turned to the ogre a split-second before it rammed into him.

Pain shot through Ben's chest. His wind exploded from his mouth.

The ogre's massive teal arms grabbed him. Squeezed him.

Hairy black arms wrapped the teal set.

The pressure lessened. Then Ben fell and hit the ground.

Snarls of the two large monsters flew on.

Blurred into one, earth and sky flip-flopped positions. Ben tumbled. The spinning horizon slowed. He came to a stop. Dizzied, he got to his knees, rocking from the continual motion in his inner ear.

"Have to recover." Ben pulled his tablet and jabbed. His finger missed the enchantment icon by millimeters on one side, then again on the second poke.

The two writhing masses of muscle struggled against each other.

Ben found tenuous equilibrium in rocking with the sway. *Got it.* His enchantment icons spread out on the screen. He ran his finger along the edge as a guide and tapped Heracles.

Recovering, Ben got to his feet.

The world leaned hard.

He leaned with it and pulled back at the last second to keep from falling over.

Seemingly wise to his attempt to balance, the world lurched the opposite direction.

From the corner of his right eye, Ben kept trying to use the Meadows Towing sign as a needle to gauge when he neared level or reached a tipping point.

He'd never find balance that way. Ben closed his eyes.

The world gave a wild buck.

Ben lowered his shoulder and swung his head the opposite way. *Even.*

The following lurches were now manageable.

He kept his focus on Bastion, the dark body in the rapidly shifting black-and-teal yinyang-ish dog-fight.

The ogre planted a foot, twisted, and heaved.

Thrown, Bastion traveled in a high arc.

Ben pressed cast. The tablet vibrated. Green energy flashed past the ogre and lit Bastion. Bastion's hair and eyes turned green as it crashed into the ground.

The ogre uttered a grunting laugh.

Ben's eyes widened.

With a grenade launcher braced on his hip, the ogre grinned like a wickedly deranged clown.

He's going to shoot.

In the vague background beyond the ogre, the hulking darkness—Bastion—got to his feet.

Ben reached out for the conjurer's bond to control Bastion, to have him do anything to help, and found a deeper connection. Disturbingly, Ben felt a union with the bestial, four-armed gorilla.

Counter to everything Ben knew about having total control of conjurations, Bastion—in the form of a slight pull on the link between them—invited Ben into it.

Thunk! A grenade wound toward him.

Forgetting about ducking, Ben winced and rode the bond into Bastion.

From Bastion's tall point of view—a good four feet higher—Ben blinked their conjoined eyes in surprise at his vanished body. *Their eyes?*

Yes.

Though Bastion didn't speak, a rough understanding donned on Ben. They occupied the same body, the same mind, but had different souls. Either one of them could give control to the other—or steal it away.

Through Bastion's senses they could smell decaying bodies under the heady bacon smell. They could hear the orcs and gorilla shuffle, struggle, and fight. The hair all over their body registered the northwest wind whistling through the scrapyard.

His Anvilsmith thumped to the earth.

The grenade flew just over the collar of the trench coat where Ben's head had been. Its riotous impact ejected shrapnel from the end of a column of cars causing the length to screech and careen.

His coat dropped to the earth covering the rest of his school uniform.

Taking control of Bastion, Ben rushed the ogre.

Spinning, it's teal index flexed on the trigger. *Thunk!*

Ben rolled to the left.

The grenade whizzed by. A dull explosion sounded behind them.

Again, the ogre's finger pulled the trigger.

Bastion pressed their four arms down. Ben recruited their powerful legs. Together, they leapt the next shot.

The ogre raised the gun toward their chest.

They were on the Krotosian.

Controlling the lower set of arms, Ben gripped the launcher, turned it away, and yanked it from the monster's hands.

Thunk! Air from the shot puffed along their gut as the grenade whistled away.

The upper set of hands—controlled by Bastion— slipped under the thick chin to wrap around the Krotosian's muscular neck.

The ogre grabbed hold of the thumbs around its neck. Leapt to plant the feet on the end of its short legs onto their torso. It extended, pulled at the thumbs to peel their grip, and started to fly away.

No! Ben took control of the upper arms and leapt after it. He caught a hold of the ogre's ankle.

In charge of the lower arms, Bastion released the weapon.

Relief washed briefly over Ben when the beast released the launcher, fading at the realization that Bastion wanted to beat and eat the monster that lorded over Meadows Towing.

Bastion tried to climb the ogre's leg.

The ogre kicked them in the face.

The impact rocked their head back. No pain. Ben kept a grip on the Krotosian.

The ogre strained as they started to descend.

Must be too much weight.

The Krotosian's purple eyes glowered. Ready to kick again, it stared down its leg.

Bastions' toes, then whole feet, touched earth.

"By Demitria!" The ogre's deep voice rumbled. "You and your family are going to be bloodspots!"

As soon as Bastions full weight registered on the earth, Ben yanked. The ogre crashed at their feet.

It made eye contact. "You hear me in there, Ben?"

How'd it know his name?

Spittle flew from its mouth as its voice turned into a growling howl. "Bloodspots!"

Bastion leapt on it.

Trying to break its jaw, Ben swung their massive fist.

The scowling, black-toothed ogre's head turned to

mist. Its violet eyes seemed to smile as the rest of its body followed suit.

Their fist wafted through. Ben relented full control to Bastion. He needed to think.

What would happen now? Was he stuck in this body? Would his just reappear when he tried to return?

Still trying to get at the ogre through its gaseous form, Bastion tromped and stomped. Unsuccessful at striking the fog, the large, four-armed gorilla switched to trying to disperse it.

Mostly undisturbed, the fog remained in the same relative loose form, as it crept across the scrapyard toward the building.

They neared his trench coat. The orb lay in the right pocket of Ben's coat, but Bastion's hands were too large to retrieve it.

With Bastion's lower arms, Ben lifted his coat.

Something akin to the initial understanding between them flashed. In it, Bastion acknowledged his plan and relented completely.

Bastion's body winked from existence.

Ben found his feet exactly where Bastion's had been. Komir's necklace, and the cool night air, pressed on his bare chest.

Sparse as always, the arm hairs on his mystically pumped arms were like thin emerald grass. The Heracles spell he had cast on Bastion remained active on him. The feeling of union... Where he and Bastion one in the same?

Ben scooped his coat, fished the Encapsulating Orb from his inner pocket, and pushed it into the fog.

Nothing happened.

He focused on the sphere to activate it. Nothing.

The fog kept rolling.

Rolling the orb in his hands, Ben lagged a step behind the Krotosian mist.

A gorilla hooted.

Ben surveyed the work bays. Two of his gorillas had managed to subdue their orcs while three stood over motionless bodies—heads either smashed or grotesquely askew.

He dismissed the idle gorillas.

As though it could tell Ben had power available to him, the Encapsulating Orb sucked at his hands.

Ben eased Argosian magic into it.

The metal sphere flashed red. Then shone a translucent silver with a liquid, mercury-like core.

Given the name Elder Komir called it, Ben figured it would only be a capturing device. Powered, the item imparted its true name—Imprisoning Orb—and abilities as a mystical prison. It wanted the user to know what the subject would go through.

Any creature tapped within would cease to age, but would be keenly aware of its surroundings. It would know the passing of time. Feel hunger. Crave drink. Slowly go mad from never-ending starvation, thirst, and loneliness.

The fog stopped and started to pool.

With full understanding of what the ogre would have to suffer through, Ben paused. Cruel and unusual punishment couldn't hold a candle to this.

Glowering violet eyes started to form in mist.

Recalling what the ogre had said. *You and your family are going to be bloodspots! You hear me in there, Ben?*

Bloodspots! Ben targeted the Krotosain with the orb and willed it to act.

In a snap, like watching video of someone exhaling smoke in reverse, the sphere sucked in all the fog.

The quarter-sized sphere expanded to the size of a softball. Along with the growth in size, the hollow-feeling orb took on the mass of a solid, steel object and started to thump in his grip.

Could the ogre be throwing itself around inside?

"You might want to hold it with both hands." Tex came from the building to stand next to him. "Your Heracles spell is about to end."

Using both hands, Ben held the orb comfortably close to his body. With pulsing thwacks, like the high-speed automatic pitcher at batting cages, the sphere spat out various items

First out, in rapid succession, three throwing knives. The grenade launcher followed. Two solid silver rings. A baton. A thick leather belt with a thicker, star-embossed plate buckle.

It stopped. *Was it over?*

A pounding from within the orb nearly wrenched it free from his grip.

Ben struggled to hold it.

A flittering golden object wrapped in Argosian energy—*the Node Key, has to be*—arced to the ground.

Chapter Thirty

TEXAS & THE NODE KEY

THE NIGHT BREEZE against his back, a building desire in his gut for a BLT, Ben leaned to examine the last item ejected from the Imprisoning Orb.

Quite fittingly, the Node Key turned out to be a skeleton key, just like in the old movies. In the base of the golden handle, a faintly pink gem lent an aesthetic balance to the two, thick, v-shaped teeth on the opposite end.

Breath hitched in his chest, Ben hoped it would disappear from here to appear wherever it belonged.

It didn't.

He closed his eyes and tried to will it to happen.

No such luck.

He'd give it some time.

As he waited for it to vanish, a warm pulse pushed into the base of his skull. Feeling like he was being watched, Ben checked over his left shoulder. The two gorillas kept the orcs in check. Over his right, only row and rows of wrecks out into the distance.

The feeling—not so different than what he felt from his fellow students when he took his time to decide what he wanted for lunch at the APA—wanted him to do something. Anything.

The annoyed patience was coming from the key.

More of a sound than a word, "Huh," escaped Ben's lips.

To his side, Tex's optics whirled and clicked to full extension before retracting with a slap. A series of small pops sounded from Ben's companion.

Ben turned.

The tiny robot's sockets went dark and it fell over. Emerald smoke, the same green as the energy in his tablet, seeped from Tex's seams.

A sudden fear—*Master Reynolds is going to revoke my gifts*—widened Ben's eyes. In the hierarchy of worst things to happen to gifts in the first week, ruining them placed slightly lower than outright losing them. "Tex?"

Ben thought the car held top spot as his favorite of the trio of gifts, but seeing his companion laying there fried, dormant, and smoking, told him otherwise. More than losing a possession, Tex's burning out weighed on his heart.

Setting the Imprisoning Orb down, Ben reached to lift Tex.

As his arms went out, the crystal at the end of the Node Key shimmered with intense sparkles.

It stole his full attention.

Everything else in the world, Tex, the gorillas, the orcs, the scrapyard, and even the Imprisoning Orb with the murderous Krotosian captured within, faded from his mind.

Using both hands, Ben lifted the key from the ground with great care.

His left hand shone red, radiating Argosian energy, while his right lay within dark Nilosian magic, anti-shining with equaled strength.

The two energies in him cajoled, begged, and demanded to be released into the key.

What Ben *should* do conflicted with what he *wanted* to do. The key had belonged to the Argosians, but the black Nilosian energy had a natural ease and flow. The Komirs had lost the key to the ogre, and he had won it from the monster. An almost alien part of him supposed that if the Argosians were strong enough in the first place, they would've kept control of the key instead of letting it fall into the Krotosian's hands.

A soft smile spread Ben's lips as he recalled learning how to channel energy atop the Suntouched Spire with Elder Komir. As though smacked away, the smile died at the vivid memory of Kograkken's sudden backhand. The giant's damning accusation—*Nilosian!*—overpowered the fond, spire-top recollection.

Ben frowned. The giant being right was worse than him being a Nilosian. He looked to the full moon and asked, "Why'd it have to be black magic?"

Distant and indiscriminant, the moon shone on.

The struggle to do what he should instead of what he wanted lessened. He'd gotten the key from the Krotosian. If the Komirs wanted to change the magic once he returned the key, that was on them.

Ben tucked the Node Key into his right coat pocket and channeled the dark, natural feeling, energy into it.

Putting the coat on properly, he buttoned it, and

stood barefoot—in what his mother called *nature-feet*—on the hard earth. Leaving the grenade launcher where it lay, he picked up the knives, rings, and baton and stashed them in his inner pockets.

Lifting the heavy belt, Ben admired the star—identical to the Meadows Towing sign—on the belt buckle. He flipped the belt over his shoulder and lifted the Imprisoning Orb.

Tex's optics twisted.

Ben turned.

Rocking slightly, his companion sat up. Focused on either the orb or the belt, Ben wasn't sure, Tex's optics whirled once then went back to their default length. "What is that?"

Ben's gaze went to the building, glancing over the five work bays to take in the overall size of the two-story building. With proper management, this place could really be something. He had heard of winning possessions during a duel, but no one had ever said stuff like this happened.

Since they'd already talked about the orb earlier, Ben patted the belt as he looked at the Meadows Towing sign with a smiling sense of ownership. "A trophy."

Tex climbed up his coat, grabbing both coat and flesh beneath to steady itself.

Ben winced as it ascended. The short must have damaged the robot's motor control or pressure setting.

Tex plopped down on his other shoulder. "I have been here before."

"Yes, Tex." Ben sighed his relief and patted his companion. "We have."

"Tex. I like that name. Is it mine?"

Holding his composure, Ben pressed his lips together to keep from showing disappointment. His companion had been reset all the way back to factory default. Would any of the old Tex, the one that had decided not to be overridden, still be in there? A ghost program maybe? Would the new Tex do the same? "It's short for Texas."

"I like Tex better."

Ben walked toward the gorillas and orcs in the work bays.

Tex asked, "What is your name, Master?"

Ben sighed at having to go through the imprinting process again. Memory of the former Tex brought a small, fond smile to his face. He'd make a concerted effort to not be sarcastic this time around. "I am Benjamin Baxter."

Chapter Thirty-One

(IN) THE END

BEN STOPPED short of entering the concrete work bays. Dark splotches crisscrossed the ground. Whether they were blood or marks from mechanic work, he didn't know. Either way, he made sure not step in any of it. The smell of old motor oil overtook the bacon aromas that had been stirring his hunger and barely covered the rotten smell from the kitchen.

Metal clinks, like wind chimes made of steel called his attention. At the feet of one of his red gorillas, wrapped from neck to ankles in chains, an orc fretted. Worry lines wrinkled its wide forehead and its wide-set eyes focused on the other conscious orc.

Curling his toes on the packed earth, Ben recalled a lesson from his mother in their garden. *Squeeze the earth, ease the tension.* It wasn't working. He turned his attention to the other orc.

Ben's other remaining gorilla held a bearded orc with its arms pinned up behind his head in a full-nelson. Both orcs wore white t-shirts and jeans. The bearded one had a Meadows Towing star ironed on over its heart.

The bearded orc bowed its head to avoid eye contact.

Still, Ben asked, "Do you speak English?"

The orc shifted its eyes to Ben's bare feet.

Ben eyed the other bound in chains. "Do you?"

It also trained its eyes on his feet.

When Ben would look at one, it would lower its eyes while the other would look at him and vice versa.

Even more annoying was not knowing if they were both male or only the one with the beard. Ben had heard some races were extremely androgynous. Could orcs be one of those races? His lips drew up and kinked with frustration. He pulled the Anvilsmith, pressed *Options* then *Translate*. Ben tapped English and scanned for a moment before finding *Orcish*. "Do you guys understand this?"

The tablet barked out a few harsh syllables.

The orcs looked to each other and back to him. Their eyes betrayed their surprise before they nodded.

The bearded one looked up a bit, but kept its eyes focused below Ben's knees. It barked a short response then let loose a string of rattling consonants.

His device had yet to start translating, but Ben picked out the words *Might-Fist* from the previous translation. "We do. If you spare our lives now, Might-Fist, we shall shed them at your whim. We will not fail you as we did Flayer Ur-Krurk."

"Ur-Krurk," Ben repeated. "The ogre?"

The bearded orc nodded.

In his head, the Nilosian energy—Bastion—looped

rapid infinity symbols. It liked being called *Might-Fist* and, to a certain extent, Ben understood why. They had defeated the Krotosian, and now all of its possessions transferred to them. It only made sense the orcs would swear allegiance to the new Might-Fist.

Bastion's elated desire proved highly infectious.

Having henchmen, in addition to controlling Meadows Towing, brought a broad grin to Ben's face.

The chained orc mewed something, which, without being translated, sounded like a heavily accented, "Let us live."

A surge of disgust bled through from Bastion and filled Ben with a firmly set disdain for the creature begging for its life. Ben pointed his tablet at the bound orc while his other hand hovered over *Cast*.

Bastion urged Ben to channel its Nilosian power to obliterate the whiner.

Ben nodded to the empathetic union-link. Toneless words—part his, mostly Bastion's—poured from his mouth. "All weakness needs to be culled."

He let the Nilosian energy travel down his arm.

Darkness engulfed his hand on the tablet, waiting to be channeled into the device. Impatient, it sizzled and flickered, sucking light from the area with each quick pulse.

The orc mewed. "I did not want to fight."

Ben spoke. His words whistled through clenched teeth. "Oh, now you speak English."

The bearded orc spoke in even tones. "Kill us or draft us. Don't allow that goblin turd to beg." It spat on the other orc. "You're skin-shame!"

"Of course, you both speak English." Ben's

Anvilsmith pinged, letting him know a translation of the term was available for him to read, but orc calling the other a *goblin turd* gave the gist of *skin-shame* without it.

"I'll take a blood-oath." The whiner stopped and started to nod. "I'm a shaman. Let me serve."

"Skin-shame! Twice more!" The bearded orc fought against the gorilla. Not prepared for the violent shift, the orc slipped free and a muted *thunk* sounded when its steel-toe cracked the other's jawbone.

Both gorillas tackled the bearded one to the concrete floor.

Pinned, the bearded orc rebuked the self-proclaimed shaman further, "Why not offer up your anus, Toad?"

The graphic insult jarred Ben's senses as a disgusted shudder rose up his spine. Whatever blasé haze that had a firm hold of him—driving him to kill the orc— vanished. Aware, he wondered how long had he been contemplating murder.

Though disgust still filled Bastion, the energy's disappointment at the lost opportunity ceased sizzling as the darkness crept back up his arm to return to its roost.

Ben made note to be extra mindful in distinguishing his feelings from Bastion's. Ben pointed to the three bodies. "Can you heal them, Toad?"

The shaman nodded emphatically. "If they're not dead."

Ben directed the gorilla to free the orc.

Toad went to the first body and pulled a knife.

Ben tensed.

Kneeling next to the fallen orc, it slid the blade across its own chest, cutting shirt and skin.

Not having a system to track the Argosian energy, Ben blinked as his two conjurations vied for what remained of the dwindling red energy. Ben suppressed a gasp as the chain-holding gorilla disappeared.

Toad threw his blade next to Ben's feet. It then removed a ring. The orc's pale outline appeared.

Ben had forgotten about his active spells.

Toad's ring sang along the concrete as it slid toward Ben. "I am bonded."

The second orc whispered, "I'll blood-oath."

Ben turned. He raised his eyebrows to the orc. "What about *your* anus?"

Its eyes dropped, searching its soul for what it would do to keep its life.

Chuckling, Ben extended his hands. "I kid. I kid."

The gorilla let go of one of the bearded orc's arms.

The orc drew the blade from its hip scabbard.

Ben's Argosian reserve ran dry. The last gorilla disappeared.

Glancing to where the gorilla had been, the bearded orc nodded once as though he and Ben had come to some kind of unspoken agreement. "You will not regret this." It put its blade away without doing the blood-oath. "I give my word as my bond."

Ben extended his hand further. "The ring?"

"It protects from divination." The orc removed the ring. Its pale aura appeared. "Might-Fist, if I flip the ring to up-end Ur-Krurk's symbol, may I still wear it?"

Remembering how Chrystal had not seen all what the scrapyard had for defense, Ben nodded to the tactical advantage the magic ring provided. He picked up the ring at his feet and noted the small crossed-axes insignia.

Ben turned to study the shaman's aura as it worked on the injured orc. It deepened to blue as it wiped its palms on the chest wound, coating its hands with blood. Except for the shaman's hands, the cobalt blue aura faded to gray. The bloody hands were aglow with the new blue energy—*how many colors of magic were there?* Ben wondered—when the shaman pressed his hands to the motionless orc. The energy poured into the body.

The orc groaned and sputtered shallow breaths.

Pointing to the last fallen orc, whose body lay chest down with its head facing up, Toad looked to Ben. "That one is beyond my magic."

THOUGH HIS HANDS still sort of ached from the boat work on the other side, Ben wanted to help bury the dead. He'd been responsible for taking their lives, he would take the blisters from working the shovel.

As they worked, the four living orcs grumbled their dissent, stating the dead's family would come for final rights. The orcs looked to one another, uncomfortable with meeting the shaman's eyes.

Toad shifted in place before stepping away to point at the belt slung over Ben's shoulder. "You act with honor, but have not donned the belt." The shaman rubbed its bloody chest.

Ben braced for a charge or a challenge. His Anvilsmith still had plenty of juice.

Toad continued, "My blood-oath is only to the rightful Might-Fist."

Ben took a few steps back, putting twenty feet—the minimal distance for a proper spell duel—between himself and the shaman. Though Bastion lay quiet, the Nilosian energy in his head began to boil. Ben's brow furrowed and his fingers ran across his SD cardholder. Two fingers came to rest on *Orion*, and one on *Shield*. "So you figure you can take it from me and claim the title for yourself?"

Extending both hands, palms out in a slow, non-threatening motion, Toad broke eye contact. The shaman focused his vision on the ground between them. "No. Not at all, but if you do not put the belt on, my blood-oath, and those bound by my blood, is null." Toad motioned to the two who he had healed. "If you refuse, we can leave when the sun rises."

Astonished Ben frown undid itself. "Why are you telling me this? You all could be free."

Toad kept his motions small and slow. "The Century of Shadows is coming, and serving a Nilosian is our only chance of surviving."

Ben bristled at indirectly being called a Nilosian. Though true enough, it didn't take away the socially programed inner-shame.

Toad continued, "You are the first human Nilosian we have seen."

Ben tightened at *Nilosian* again, but not quite as hard this time.

"You say we could be free, but life for an orc is never

that simple." Toad motioned to the orcs and pointed to the belt again. "We serve the strongest. We have always served the strongest. You have proven to be the strongest here. You are human, and humans are rumored to reward loyalty." Again, the orcs nodded along with the shaman who bowed his head. "We want to be rewarded."

While Ben hadn't planned to put the belt on, he wondered how they could've not been rewarded before now. They must've been thanked before—even if in some weird ogre-ish custom. Then he recalled that there were four other bullet points under the Orcish words for shame-feast.

All four orcs looked at him with honest yearning.

Ben pulled the heavy belt from his shoulder. He ran his fingers over the large buckle, letting his fingertips explore the embossed grooves. He traced the star.

"I want to record this." Tex said, pinching him as it climbed down from his shoulder. "May I?"

"Yes, Tex." Ben held the buckle with both hands at shoulder height. The wide leather strap meant to go around him folded over its length on the ground. "Please do."

Tex backed up until he stood inline with the orcs. "Ready."

Ben wrapped the belt around his waist. Aside from it shrinking to fit him, nothing special happened. He shrugged at Toad. "It's on."

The relief amongst their faces was like finding out the hardest test of the school year was one of those trick quizzes where you only had to put your name on it.

Ben asked, "Better?"

Toad and the two he healed nodded. The bearded orc gave him a thumbs up.

———

ALMOST FOUR WEEKS had passed and the orcs had made serious progress on cleaning the inside of the Meadows Towing building. Though the smell of rancid meat smothered in rotten cheese lingered, the sources had been mostly removed. Still, more years of crap had yet to be discarded. Clean as they might, nothing short of new carpet, tile, and paint would bring Meadows Towing's customer center back into acceptable standards.

Due to overwhelming homework, Ben chose late Saturday nights to visit. He'd have most of his weekend homework done and the orcs wouldn't be there to see him checking their paperwork.

Ben didn't want to sneak, but their arguments against his decision to shut down the chop shop arm of Meadows Towing made him suspicious. Their lives were easier when stolen cars were brought to them. Now they were busy doing legitimate tows.

He liked to think that without a place to unload, car theft across the Vegas Valley would drop.

Part of him wondered what the *Mystique* made the orcs look like as they serviced those who were not starwise. The same part of him wanted to take an orc to his parents' house to watch the mundane neighbors react.

Ben closed the filing cabinet, wrote the *Mystique*

question at the bottom of his checklist, and continued his musings as he got back in his car.

Now, all he had to do was see if Pepperjacks had reopened so he could return the Node Key. Oddly, the supper club had been repaired, but remained closed with mystical barring like he'd never seen. Still, he'd drive by and check. Then he'd watch the recording on him becoming the first human Might-Fist of Meadows Towing before heading off to the Samhain festival.

Pleased as usual with his inspection, Ben started his car, and drove away with a smile. He began to plan the party for the orcs to reward their hard work and help them to celebrate Halloween.

ABOUT THE AUTHOR

Ezekiel James Boston hales from Las Vegas and currently resides in the Pacific Northwest. Favoring fantasy, science fiction, and paranormal occult, he's authored over a hundred short stories, a score of short novels, and half a dozen full length novels.

Aside from being an avid writer, Ezekiel enjoys reading and games of all sorts. He chose to give up "active" sports after jamming his fingers and discovering that an author cannot slam their forehead onto the keyboard and have the story appear on the screen.

For exclusive content, please visit:

ezekieljamesboston.com/subscribe-to-ejb/

ALSO BY EZEKIEL JAMES BOSTON

Novels:

Birthday Bedlam: Book One

Samhain Shenanigans: Book Two

Yuletide Yield: Book Three

Novelette:

Nexus Bar & Grill: A World of Benjamin Baxter Starwise
Novelette

Short stories:

Gateway Blood, Buck Tales

Soul Survivor, Buck Tales

Jamal & the Skeleton's Heart, Buck Tales

Collections:

Benjamin Baxter — Darkness Within Trilogy

COMING SOON

Samhain Shenanigans, Book Two of The Darkness Within Trilogy

PLEASE NOTE: Word of mouth is crucial for any author to succeed. If you enjoyed this book, please consider rating it or leaving a review where you purchased... Even if it's just a line or two.

Thank you for reading.

www.ingramcontent.com/pod-product-compliance
Lightning Source LLC
Chambersburg PA
CBHW022101170626
46808CB00002B/542

* 9 7 8 1 6 2 5 3 8 0 5 1 7 *